Through the Night

Edward Martin III

Published by **Hellbender Media**

rare and voracious entertainment

HellbenderMedia.com

Cover painting by Mindy Reinke
Cover design by Leslie Herzfeld
First edition, released August 2014

Tiu libro estas dediĉita al tiuj,
kiuj estas skolta antaŭen:

Edward Takeshi Martin
Ronald Bruce
Steve Fleming
Lisa A. Box
Mark Bourne

Mi esperas ke viajn vojaĝojn estas plena de paco kaj lumo!
Vi estas maltrafis kare.

Table of Contents

The Fabric Is Large..1
The Canister Finds A Home... 2
The Wolf, Confused, Runs.. 3
The Farmer Chases 4
The Family Might Be Lost.. 5
Erin Hides It From Meredith 7
Seems Like An Easy Walk... 9
It's Not Entirely Sure 12
The Farmer Closes In... 13
The Last Ditch 14
There's Just Not Enough Traction 16
Mistakes Are Always Possible.. 18
Good Samaritans 19
Last Thoughts 21
Nuts 22
First Aid... 24
Not All Of The Birds 28
Sleeping Dogs 29
Erin Makes Her Point 32
The Solution To A Family Problem.. 35
The Iron Fails 40
The Lucky Couple 41
Sundown 43
Mark Catches Up 44
Like Shadows 45
A Family Reunion.. 46
Underground Might Have Been Better 50
She Discovers Her Limitations 52
The Gray Tide.. 53
She Discovers One of Their Limitations.. 54
Family Has Limits, Too.. 56
Jake Sets Some Ground Rules 59
Riding On Fumes 62
Place Your Bets 64
Never Judge A Book 65
A Cautious Meeting... 66
The Cougar 68
Suddenly Thick 69
A New Company.. 73
An Exit Is Planned 75
Some Parts May Be Damaged During Shipment... 77
You Can't Always Get What You Want. 81
It's A Matter Of Rhythm 82
The Open Sky.. 85
Better Than Nothing 86
It's The Quiet Ones 87
Jake Finds One Possible Solution... 89
Introductions Are A Form Of Medicine, Too. 92
Knowing When To Hold 'Em 96
Mark Gets Lucky 97
Electrons, More Or Less...100
So Much for Navigation 104
Better Late Than Never 105
Reassessing 106
Tick-Tock 107
No Signal...108
Supposed To Be A Security Feature 110

Double-Checking 112
More Planning... 113
"It's How We Keep Everything From Happening All At Once."............ 114
Frame of Reference 115
Briefly Unmonitored.. 117
Dominance Games.. 118
Whispers 120
Man Cave.. 122
In The Heart 124
Pawns 128
The Word 129
Over His Head 131
Orders 133
In The Wrong Hands 134
Remembering The Bei Chez Heinz 135
Trail of Destruction 137
More Echoes 138
Pure Evil, Man. Pure Fuckin' Evil. 139
Priority Observations 141
The Facts Of The Matter 142
The Back Door... 144
All Signs Point To Bad 145
Every Dance Has A Why 146
Strange Bedfellows 147
Built Wolf-Tough 148
He Who Hesitates Is... 149
Carpet Bombing 150
Peasant Under Glass 151
Flanked 152
Still On Plan A 154
A Very Special Bullety Event 155
Super Effective 157
Clever Girl 158
Sometimes People Just Change 159
Silence Is Golden... 161
Going Home 163
The Problem 164
To Rest 165
Assume A Spherical Cow 166
Something's In The Bag 171
Dark Santa 173
Coke Does Not Technically Add Life 175
Hit Or Miss 177
The Terrible Twos Come Early 178
Family Business.. 180
Carnage 183
Shock The Monkey 184
Heavy Petting 185
Vows... 187
The Problem With Sunlight 189
Watchers 191
Listeners... 192
Mourners 193
The End Of The Song 194
Locked In, Locked Out, Locked Up 195
The Eye Of The Storm 197
Regular Checkups.. 198
Honey... 199
Triple-X 200

ICU 202
The Abyss Gazes Back 203
"My Hand is Steady, My Eyes Keen." 204
Carpet 206
Heads I Lose 207
Shreds 209
Echoes Again 210
Words Sometimes Fail 211
Shift Change 212
Going To Ground 214
End Of The Rainbow 216
The Setup Comes Before The Punchline 217
Phase Two 220
When It's A Jar 223
Pretty Dancing Lights 224
Phase Three 225
Packing Up 226
A Layered Approach 227
Tranquility 229
Deadly Thread In A Dirty Needle 231
Focus On Low Impact 232
Dimension Z 234
Uphill, Downhill, Bing-Bang-Boom 235
Taking A Breather 236
The Coefficient of Static Friction 237
Only Solutions 238
The Diamond 241
Studying For The Finals 242
In The Moist Dark Places Filled With Things That Creepeth 245
Light Gambling 247
A Definite Sense Of Unexpected Intimacy 248
Re-Org 249
One Man's Trash 250
The Skipper 252
A Dark Silence In The Dark Noise 253
Crossroad Sweetening 254
Crashing Waves 255
Special Deliverance 257
Reunion 259
Short Circuited 260
Zero Contact 261
Closure 262
Tongue of Flame 264
Benediction 265
Walkers 266
The Publisher 267
The Author 268
The Last Word 269

The Fabric Is Large

To understand the vastness of space requires a remarkable mind and most of the minds of Earth are simply not up to the task. This is where a whale can travel one quarter of the planet's circumference and have that referred to as "an extraordinary trek." In such limited frameworks, a light-year is mind-bogglingly far, and multiple light-years makes no sense at all.

This does not mean there aren't other species who do understand better the kinds of distances involved in traveling from one star to another. There are quite a few, in fact, considering how vast space really is.

Most of these species are fairly decent, having achieved technological advancement in the same measure as social maturity.

Most of them.

The Canister Finds A Home

The canister spun through the darkness. Its body was scratched and pitted and scored by micrometeorites, by random blasts of gamma radiation, and by having been traveling in space for so long.

The payload remained safe inside the dull stone body.

The payload was an organic machine, chilled and dormant for the journey through cold space, but otherwise alive. Its mental function was low and vegetative, but even in that state, given the length of time it had flown through space, it had arrived at the most stunning realization of its life.

It was bored.

The canister had traveled through space longer than most modern species of life on Earth had existed, in a line woven between the gravitational paths of stars. Its destination had not been a specific planet orbiting a specific sun. It was launched with sophisticated sensing equipment and an AI clever enough to aim it once it located a suitable target. That was all in the past, however, as many onboard systems had broken down.

Now, the canister was simply a container. The container protected its primitive occupant, but it no longer operated in accordance with its original plan. It had improvised.

A large silvery satellite crossed the canister's path, its surface reflecting a blinding white light. Below the canister and beyond the satellite lay a blue planet, with green and brown and white highlights.

Gravity turned the canister's path and it curved down, entering the thin atmosphere.

It glowed as layers of thicker air flew past. Pieces flaked off and vaporized.

This looked to be the place.

The Wolf, Confused, Runs

Not fair, not fair, the wolf thought as it ran.

The chicken coop had been left open. If the door had been closed, if the pen gate had been closed, it would have moved on, but the gate was open and the door was open. There was no denying it.

Those chickens belonged to him.

The air behind it cracked and chips flew from a nearby tree. The Man was angry.

The wolf zigged off to a side path and kept running. Once it was out of the denser brush, it would make better time. Plus, it didn't know this area, so that was a huge disadvantage. The valley had steep walls and on occasion, the wolf into against impassable stone.

Patches of sunlight flashed and flickered through the tree canopy as the wolf jumped and ran.

Another report, this time the bullet flying off into the woods.

The wolf jumped through brush onto another path, and kept running.

Totally not fair.

The Farmer Chases

Jonah ran like crazy through the woods.

Nine chickens, he thought. *Nine chickens in less than the ten minutes it took for him to go get the wheelbarrow and bring it back. That wolf came right into the pen, right into the coop and killed nine chickens.*

Jonah's fury was understandable. Six were good layers and the other three were scheduled for this weekend's roadside market. That's real money and they were already running short this season.

So he ran like a beast after the thing. Every time it was in the open long enough to get a bead, he aimed and fired. He might not hit it, but he would at least confuse it with the shots. A confused wolf could be shot. A shot wolf wouldn't eat any more chickens. And then he'd have a chance at breaking even this year.

The Family Might Be Lost

The RV crawled along the dirt road at four miles per hour. It didn't seem right to refer to such slow speeds in miles per hour, but that was the going rate.

This section was open enough that Burke could see around the road. Trees, brush, and the occasional rough clearing, but nothing that suggested a campsite. Branches and twigs scrabbled against the sides of the RV as he mollycoddled it over the road.

Mollycoddling an RV is no small task, particularly on an unpaved road. He stared ahead, concentrating on every foot they travelled.

Sue sighed.

He spared a quick glance over to her, and then brought his eyes back on the road.

Burke loved his wife. Oh sure, not everything was hunky dory all the time, but that was part of the marriage business, right? You basically loved each other and if you had static, then you solved it and moved on.

When he looked at her, he realized that his own sweat wasn't solely the product of nervousness. He had been focusing so much on the road that he hadn't realized the cabin was hot.

Her long brown hair, which normally bounced out a bit from her head, lay slick against her forehead. Her tank top was browner than he remembered.

"Hon, could you kick the AC up a bit?" he asked. Except that as he said "bit," the front left tire dropped into a rut, and it came out sounding like "Bi-eya-it."

Sue leaned forward and fiddled with the AC controls. "It's already 65," she said. "You told me before you didn't think going any colder would work."

He nodded his head. He had to – they hit another bump.

"Yeah," he muttered. "Even with the partition closed, it wouldn't get colder. Sorry."

She leaned back and looked out the window.

5

"We're a little off the beaten path," she said. "You know that, right?"

The RV bucked again in response.

"I'm using the map Larry gave us," he said.

"I know, it's just that he didn't tell us we would be four-wheeling the RV."

"I'll talk with him Tuesday," said Burke.

The RV lurched again.

"See if he'll chip in on new shocks," said Sue. "Yellowstone wouldn't have been like this."

"I promise we'll do Yellowstone next year. But we had these great mountains and this great valley right down the highway..."

"... and Larry is all about the adventure and the exploring and the having fun in the wilderness."

Burke grinned.

"Besides," he added, "this is a great chance to get away from it all, for us to go out and be a family all by ourselves in the woods, without TVs or Internet or phones or anything."

"Great," she laughed. "Just what I need. A horror movie."

Erin Hides It From Meredith

Despite the bouncing of the RV, Erin was able to keep her place on the bed while reading. A lot of her friends said they couldn't read while in a car, but she couldn't imagine *not* reading. Anywhere. Besides, it helped to be lying next to a window. She didn't see any of the trees or bushes or road, only the almost-overhead sky. It was a stable object she could keep track of. Clouds didn't dash and zip around like trees and bushes did.

The RV hit a big bump and she felt herself bounce up from the bed.

She had an advantage. She weighed about a pound and a half. Her clothes probably weighed more than she did.

She tried to not giggle when they bounced. It would be unseemly. Years of practice allowed her to keep her face neutral and frowny no matter what. Between that and the black clothes, she had been able to prevent most people from bothering her, which was what she wanted in the first place.

Because people, given the opportunity, sucked.

Across the RV, braced between the little formica table and the built-in seats, sat Erin's older sister Meredith. Meredith was the opposite of Erin in every way that mattered. Meredith was blonde, Erin's hair was black. Meredith was round-cheeked and bubbly, Erin wasn't gaunt, but if she had been eighty years old, she would be called gaunt. Now, it was more like people worried she wasn't eating enough. Not round-cheeked and bubbly. No way. Meredith dressed in bright colors and liked to play with others. Again, Erin failed on both those counts.

Meredith glared back at her sister.

Ah, that was something they had in common. A mutual hatred of everything the other stood for.

That's what sisters are for, apparently.

From her position, Erin's eye caught a flash outside. She looked up.

7

Whatever it was, it burned bright, like a flare. White and bits of red and green and yellow fire streaked off it as it tumbled and fell across the sky. It was gorgeous and terrifying at the same time. It was also silent. This part impressed her the most – that whatever this huge flaming thing was, it made no sound.

"Cool," she muttered. Sometimes she lost track of the fact that she was supposed to be nonplussed.

"What?" asked Meredith.

Erin glanced down at her sister, then back up to the sky. Where the falling thing had flashed, there was only a vapor trail.

She pulled the book back to her face.

"Nothing," she said. "Just the sky."

"The sky?"

"It's blue. That's cool."

Seems Like An Easy Walk

Jake stopped splitting wood, waiting for his own echoes to die down. He loved the smell of a Douglas fir forest. There was nothing like it on Earth and he never tired of it. That smell was damp and wet and homey. It filled him with memories of when he was a child, which was an impossibly long time ago. The forest smelled the same now as it did then.

He listened, and he could hear all the tiny little sounds of a living forest. Unseen things scampering around on beds of needles in the dark undergrowth. Soft whisperings where the wind blows through the trees. A crow calling out, making noise for the fun of it.

He opened his eyes and took it all in.

The cabin lived in its own clearing, but surrounding it were firs that towered high enough to make the clearing absurdly vertical, almost surreal by comparison. The road wasn't perfect, but it was serviceable, and it wound through the trees and off into the distance. It didn't continue onward, either, because Jake's cabin was the end of the line.

Well, Jake and Lucy's cabin.

He glanced at the front door. It was wide and thick and open a bit. A wisp of smoke drifted downward from the chimney and filled his nostrils with his second favorite smell ever – a wood fire.

Now that his eyes took in his home, his ears picked up another sound. Dishes clinking against each other while being washed. Dinner had been, as usual, fantastic.

He sighed again and looked up.

He saw it before he heard it. It flashed in the sky, spitting white light and other bits and pieces of colored light as it burned up. It spiraled a little, but tore a hole right through the blue early evening sky.

A faint hissing came from it, but it wasn't a hissing he had ever heard before. It wasn't a teakettle or a snake. This was a dangerous burning hissing.

9

It cleared the trees – it was that high – but not much more. Jake followed with his eyes, even past the trees. He knew the woods enough to know where it was, even when it disappeared, hidden in the green.

He listened with intent as the hissing grew distant. He had a feeling it wouldn't be quiet for long.

Three seconds after the hissing grew past his ability to hear, he heard a different sound, a burst of crackling. It lasted less than a second, but even in that small frame of time, he knew what it was. Any man who had been in a forest in any sort of storm grew to fear the sound of trees shattering.

The sound blossomed into a rolling thunderous boom, and then a clap of impact so loud it shook the ground.

Jake looked down. In his hand, he still held the splitting maul.

He stared through the impenetrable trees. He calculated in his head. Three seconds overheard, a second longer of hitting trees, and then impact. He worked out the timing.

"Lucy," he called out. The sound of dishes stopped.

Lucy came to the door, wiping her hands on her pants.

Back when Jake lived in the world, he used to imagine that there were demons and that celebrities made success-deals with them. All celebrities got their status from the deal. Some made better deals, though, and managed to swing "looks good" as part of that deal.

Lucy wasn't a celebrity, but she had obviously swung the right kind of deal. Even at 55, she was a looker, with long auburn hair, green eyes, cheeks that seemed custom-built for smiling, and a rugged toughness that was rare in a woman. Jake considered himself lucky to have caught her eye in the first place, and grateful she'd chosen to hitch her wagon to an old Wobblie like him.

"Come out and take a look at this," he said.

She stepped out and looked up, following his finger.

He told her what he saw, although the sky revealed only a dissipating contrail.

"About a mile away," she said. "Out by our rock."

He nodded. "I was thinking that. You want to go check it out?"

She grinned. "I'll get our packs." She turned and trotted inside.

"Lucy," he said.

She stopped and turned back.

He gave the woods another look, considered a thought, and then settled. "Could you also grab my shotgun while you're in there?"

For a moment, she paused, and then stepped into the darkness of the cabin.

It's Not Entirely Sure

Smoke hung in the air. The trees hadn't burned, but a ragged cylindrical hole burrowed through the branches, from the canopy down through the range of the leaves, and deep into the ground near a thin game trail.

A crater gashed open, ten feet in diameter, bordered with burnt salal, charred fir leaves, and smoking loamy earth.

It could see, in a way. It could see the long distant patch of blue sky still visible through the hole in the canopy. It could see the smoke everywhere. It could see the floating bits of burning vegetation. It could see the cracked boundaries of its canister, the thing that had sheltered it on its ancient journey.

It could also see itself, unfolding. It could see its own surface filling with an atmosphere rich in nitrogen, tinged with oxygen. It could feel glands reviving, sacs filling, and limbs unfurling. Yes, definitely limbs.

It was not designed for this kind of atmosphere, but that was acceptable. It wasn't designed for any one particular kind of atmosphere, but its kind tended to adapt. As much and as long as was necessary.

It continued unfolding, breathing, and waiting.

The Farmer Closes In

I've got you, he thought.

Jonah's legs were burning up, but he could see that damn wolf ahead of him. He could practically feel it already. Closer, closer, closer...

One hand kept the shotgun at the ready, because he knew the wolf would hit another dead-end and then instead of running, it would turn around facing him with all teeth pointing outward.

So, his hands were ready. His arms were ready.

But his legs pushed harder. His long legs stretched, eager to close.

The Last Ditch

The wolf felt the Man close behind.

It did not enjoy the thought of confronting him. Most unwise. Besides, the wolf wasn't a fighter. That's why it ate chickens.

Which were officially free, as the gates were all open, it added. *Not that that mattered to the Man.*

Running Time was almost over, and then something was going to have to change.

Then something changed.

The path jinked around a corner and the wolf saw a pit ahead. That was new.

In that split second, it knew it had a chance. There were many things a Man could do that a wolf couldn't. A Man could work tools. A Man could operate machines. A Man could open gates.

But a Man couldn't jump.

Not like a wolf, anyway.

It threw down a final burst of speed and launched itself from the edge of the pit.

The instant the wolf left the ground, it knew – absolutely knew in the way that all animals know for certain – two things.

First, it knew that until it had finished its landing, it was vulnerable. The Man had a gun, and the wolf in mid-leap was exposed. But the Man was running, too, and that could confound things. Which would be good.

Second, it knew that if it did make the other side of the pit, then it was home free. The jump was executed perfectly. The wolf was at exactly the right arc, going exactly the right speed, and his feet were in exactly the right place. As long as nothing happened, he would land exactly where he planned, twelve feet from his launch point, and in full-speed stride.

What the wolf *didn't* know was what happened instead.

It felt something around its foot. Something thin and strong. Had it snagged a vine as it leaped? *But the path was clear!*

Then it felt the ground, as it spun, yanked out of its perfect jump and downward with a tremendous force, onto its back.

The wolf lay confused a moment, then sprang to its feet.

Except it didn't.

In fact, the ground beneath it didn't even feel like ground.

It felt like roots. Moving roots. Something twisting and writhing.

Then the wolf felt more thin, twisting things wrapping themselves around its paws and its belly and even its neck.

It howled once, as the burning started, and then three more tentacles flowed down its throat and the sky cracked and the darkness rushed in.

There's Just Not Enough Traction

Jonah spun around the corner right behind the wolf, just as it jumped.

Godammit!

Still running, he raised the shotgun. He might not have the best chance to hit it, but he was going to at least wing the damn thing. He knew that much.

The wolf floated in the air and crossed Jonah's sight.

Jonah squeezed the trigger.

In the slice of time between the squeezing of the trigger and the bucking of the shotgun, Jonah saw something he had never seen before.

A grey rope rose from the ground and wrapped itself around the wolf in mid-air. In the same motion, it tightened, pulling the wolf down and out of sight.

The shotgun bucked against Jonah's shoulder, but there was no wolf.

He raised the barrel and looked, then caught sight of the wolf in the bottom of the pit.

His feet danced a different dance than the triumphant catch-the-wolf dance they had danced moments ago. Now they danced a stop-running dance. No, more frantic. A go-in-reverse dance.

Jonah's brain realized that no matter how hard the legs worked, they weren't going to win this one – he was moving too fast. There was only one thing to do and no time left.

Jonah dropped flat on his ass, skidding along the needle-covered trail.

He slid four feet before coming to a halt, which was two feet further than the lip of the crater. As his hips went over, he clawed at the ground, and his legs bicycled hard to pitch his lower half back to ground level, back to where things made sense, back to where he didn't have to share a smoking hole in the ground with something that his brain still didn't want him to remember seeing.

His fingers caught in the trail dirt and his body stopped sliding. The muscles of his shoulders and arms popped, but he yanked his hips back to solid ground and scrabbled hard to keep retreating.

He felt his feet cross the threshold of the crater and then launched himself away, but somehow, between the think and the do, that isn't what happened. He stretched long, and his ankles were pulled out from under him.

He spun in midair and, in a surreal second, he saw his shotgun fly from his fingers and spiral away.

In the first bounce of the shotgun against the ground, Jonah felt something gripping both his legs below the knees. Something that felt like steel cables. Something that moved.

In the second bounce of the shotgun, the cables had wrapped themselves around his chest and his left arm.

The third bounce of the shotgun was the end of its flight, and at that moment, Jonah felt the grip boil up his neck.

As something moist and muscular pulled his eyes shut, he realized that his last sight on earth was the barrel of his shotgun kicking up a little burst of muddy dirt and pine needles.

That's a shame, he thought. *I thought for sure I would—*

And then he also was gone.

Mistakes Are Always Possible

It wasn't sure what to do.

Normally, it used the first sample, but in this case, it had two samples. Two samples were unprecedented.

The process was inevitable, but there was some measure of control possible. Two samples.

Chemistry was happening. Physics was happening. Microscopic organic factories were revving and firing off in a sequence that had been planned for half a million years.

It must decide what to do. Both samples were being assessed. Both samples were being broken down. But it was designed to work with one, to work with the primary form, the initial sample. That was the design and that was all the resources available to it.

But both were being conformed. Both were being assimilated.

This could not be allowed to continue. If it continued, then there would be no material remaining to complete the process, and that would be a fundamental breakdown of the mission.

But it was proceeding anyway, whether or not sufficient material existed.

A resource crisis was seconds away.

It wasn't a complicated thinker. It didn't have a complicated task that required many steps. It was a simple organism, with a simple mission. The brains were all in the canister AI, which had perished in a micrometeor strike eighty thousand years ago. Since then, it had been alone, with nothing but its own intellectual levels against which it might compare itself.

So, under the circumstances, it's natural that it might make a mistake. Only natural.

It compromised.

Good Samaritans

"We *are* going to camp soon, right?" asked Cindy as she pulled herself over the ancient nurse log that lay across the game trail.

"Sure, sure," said Gene. "I was thinking maybe another hour, unless we find ourselves a nice little clearing. You know, something soft and flat where we can pitch a tent and no one will bother us."

She nodded and landed on the ground. Cindy didn't like being muddy without having plumbing nearby. A bathroom, a toilet, a shower. All of those things were important. All of those things were wonderful. She loved showering. Especially when she was muddy, showering was sublime. But there was no shower out here in Hatchet Valley. No showers, no toilets, and probably not even a running stream where she could soak her feet.

It wasn't that she was a wimp. She really wasn't. She just hated being dirty.

She glanced at Gene, ten feet away, who was brushing moss off his legs. She enjoyed his legs. In fact, the whole package was nice.

Correction, she hated being dirty in *some* ways.

"But we're on a ridge," she said. "Do they even *have* clearings on ridges?"

He grinned at her. "Sure, if there's a game trail, then there's going to be a place where—"

A shot interrupted him.

They both froze, staring at each other.

"Did you hear that?" she asked.

He spun his head. "Did you get a direction on it?"

She tried to think, tried to compare ears, but nothing came out. She shook her head. "Sorry," she whispered, still listening.

"Maybe there'll be another."

Then they heard the scream. It wasn't a cautious scream. It wasn't a hesitant scream. It was a desperate scream.

"Over there!" shouted Gene and he ran down a side trail.

19

For a moment, Cindy felt a chill of dread, as if this was a much worse idea than she ever could have known. But that was silly thinking. Someone needed help, and she and Gene were going to help.

She pulled her pack close and ran after him.

Last Thoughts

The compromise was a compromise. It wasn't elegant, but it solved the problem.

Things were progressing.

The chemistry was working, although it wasn't what should be happening.

The base unit was growing and the raw materials were being taken from both samples. It was causing some fabrication issues, but the chemical cascades were robust and adjusting their process.

Shifts and changes.

There was a little tug of consciousness.

It felt something it had never felt before. It felt a tug on itself. On its own mind.

It tried to ask what was happening, but the question dissolved mid-stream.

Realization struck as the first barrier broke down.

Normally, it would remain conscious throughout the conversion process, but the compromise had broken that plan.

The compromise was more sophisticated and also more unpredictable than it had foreseen. The compromise needed more than raw materials. It needed a mind. It needed some sort of consciousness.

There was only one available.

It didn't even have time to feel sad as it was ripped apart.

Nuts

Squirrels have a short attention span.

Eight minutes ago, an impact blast had terrified this squirrel. Five minutes ago, a wolf had terrified this squirrel. Four minutes ago, an errant blast from a dead man's shotgun had terrified this squirrel.

But that was all in the past. Now it was time to look for pinecones.

Pinecones were delicious and had sweet bits inside them.

Something had knocked a lot of pinecones off the firs, and the squirrel loved it. Not that pinecones were hard to collect – they hung on the tree branches until they dropped. But these were perfect pinecones, because they were ready to drop, but hadn't dropped yet.

Until now.

And they were delicious.

The squirrel heard a crackling in the nearby pit and hopped over to take a look. Maybe there were pinecones in the hole.

There were no pinecones. There was something else in the hole. Something pink and wet.

The squirrel cocked its head to one side in curiosity. Curiosity was unusual for a squirrel, but not all squirrels were alike.

The pink wet thing was wriggling around like something in a bag. It crackled and whispered and made slithery noises against the raw churned earth and the wet slurry of shredded meat in which it nested.

It grew.

As it grew, the pile of flesh and muscle and bone around it shrunk, sucked into the glob as it swelled into a new shape.

Beneath the translucent surface membrane, differentiation occurred at an astounding rate. Anatomy formed and reformed – bones, sinews, flesh, and fur. For a moment, a flat-faced skull opened its mouth in a silent scream, and then it was dissolved again, and replaced by a different skull, one that had a longer

22

face. Flat teeth appeared, were reabsorbed, and then replaced by longer pointed teeth.

The embryo grew larger, man-sized, and the differentiation was complete. Beneath the surface, thick fur twitched in time with growing muscles, and the skin strained and stretched to contain the creature. Broad dark hands clenched and unclenched, pushing outward. The skull elongated, the teeth extended, and the large eyes grew more distinct.

Claws strained against the membrane and then, with a soft snap, it split open. The creature rolled and kicked and mewled and vomited fluids and remnants of the development process.

At the sound, the squirrel suddenly realized it had enough pinecones, and vanished behind a log.

First Aid

Cindy crashed through the brush a few seconds behind her boyfriend.

"Hello? Hello?" Gene called out.

There was no answer.

"We have First Aid!" she shouted. "Can you hear us?" As soon as she said it, she realized how dumb it sounded. *We have first aid.* Did they think people would be carrying something else? *We brought biscuits and Jenga.* Happens all the time.

Gene looked at her. "You hear anything?"

She stopped and listened. The trees around them whispered with the wind, and there were sounds, but they were ordinary sounds.

"No," she shook her head. "I don't hear anything."

Gene was concentrating. "I thought I heard something," he said. "Someone moaning. Just before you got here."

"It wasn't me."

"I know, I know." He listened again, and she did, too.

Something was moving around in the brush nearby.

"You hear that?" he whispered.

She nodded.

"Hey, hey, are you okay," he called out. "We're here to help. We don't mean you any harm. Can you speak? Can you make a noise?"

He stepped further down the path, listening, and stumbled.

"It's a gun," Cindy said.

A shotgun lay on the ground. Clods of dirt spotted it. Gene picked it up. Smelled the muzzle. Nodded to her.

Another couple of steps and they were at the lip of the crater.

"Jesus," she said. "What the hell happened here?"

Gene leaned down, then jumped inside.

"You remember that hissing sound?" he asked. "A little before we heard the shot? I'll bet this was it. I'll bet it's a meteorite."

She looked at the trees around. Patches of leaves still smoked.

Something smelled funny. Sour.

She looked down at Gene. The sour smell was stronger.

"Check out what I found," he said, as he climbed out of the crater.

At the end of the shotgun hung something wet and membranous.

"It looks like a skin or something," he said.

She peered at it, but didn't touch it. When she was a little girl, she lived on a horse ranch east of Phoenix. One afternoon, their mare foaled. Prior to that, she – as with all little girls – loved horses and ponies and thought of them as magical. That afternoon, though, as she stood holding a garbage bag while her mother shoveled afterbirth into it for the vet, The Horror of Biology replaced all those dreams. Every once in a while, she still had dreams of that afterbirth, squirming and jellylike.

That was what it looked like, the thing Gene dangled from the end of the shotgun.

"That looks like—" she started to say, but something hot and wet splashed her in the face.

She blinked.

The gun wobbled, and then it and its grotesque cargo dropped to the ground.

Stunned, Cindy looked at her boyfriend.

His expression was unlike anything she'd ever seen before. She'd seen him surprised. She'd seen him outraged. She'd seen him shocked. But this was all three, plus something else. Her eyes traveled down and she saw what had happened.

Her first thought was *How silly – I didn't think he could suck in his stomach that much. What a party trick.* Then she realized it wasn't sucked in. It was gone.

Gene's torso had been torn open.

25

The shotgun still hung from his right hand, its muzzle once again in the dirt, but his left hand fluttered across where his stomach used to be, patting, feeling, crawling like an independent thing.

She blinked and a red film dripped across her left eye. She wiped it away and her hand came back slick with blood. She looked at it, then back at Gene.

The wound was turning dark around the edges.

Slowly, slowly, he fell to his knees.

Then, his left hand fell away and everything else that luck or chance held in fell out and landed on the ground in front of him.

His eyes unfocused, his mouth worked without noise, and then Gene fell. He twitched once, then twice, and then was still.

Cindy had not realized she was holding her breath until the first sudden inhalation of shock.

Something moved behind him and she looked up.

She thought it was a dog. Then she thought it was a wolf. Then she realized she was wrong.

It crouched on all fours but was still the size of a pony. Shaggy damp gray hair covered its body except for a white streak up its face.

It rose up.

It stood on his hind legs, seven feet tall.

Cindy found herself staring at its paws.

Not paws.

It had hands. Fingers. Almost human fingers, except that each was hairy and tipped with long nails. One of the hands dripped with blood.

She looked into its face.

As she did, it shook its massive head, and snatched from the air a stray hanging gobbet of meat.

"Gene...?" she said. It was all she could think of to say.

The beast looked at her and she looked into its eyes. The eyes were not animal eyes. They flashed and reflected in ways she had never seen before. A bit golden and a bit green.

She felt the skin prickle all along the back of her head and neck.

She almost thought to run, but before she could finish the thought, those jaws opened wide and flew at her.

Not All Of The Birds

The screaming lasted only a few seconds.

The crows stopped eating. They hopped, fluttering their wings. One flew away from the tree above the crater. The rest paused a few seconds, their heads sideways while their featureless black eyes observed the scene on the ground.

Then they continued eating.

It was that time of the night.

Sleeping Dogs

The tent unzipped.

Kate slipped in, and shook Eddie's leg.

"Eddie," she whispered.

He lay, desperately clinging to sleep. It had been a nice dream. There had been some clowns. And a merry-go-round. He could still hear the music.

"Eddie!"

The music dissolved into the sounds of his wife.

He opened his eyes. The late afternoon sun filtered blue through the tent skin. He felt underwater.

"What?" he asked.

"Did you hear that?" Kate asked him.

"Hear what? I didn't hear anything."

"I heard screaming."

"Screaming?" He sat up on his elbows. "Hon, there's no one out here but us."

"I heard screaming," she said. "I'm sure of it. A girl."

Eddie sighed. He sat up. "You think you heard a scream?"

"I know it," she said.

"But we're alone."

"I know what I heard. C'mon, could you check it out?"

"I'm sleeping. You check it out."

She grabbed him. "Eddie, I'm serious. Could you please check it out?"

He eyed her. She looked serious.

"I'm scared," she said. "I know we're supposed to be alone, but I heard it and now I don't know what it is and please could you go look. Please?"

Eddie nodded. "Sure," he said. He leaned forward and crawled out. "Maybe it was a cougar or something. They're supposed to sound like people when they hunt."

"I don't think it was a cougar," she said.

"Do you know what a cougar sounds like?" he asked.

"I don't think this was a cougar," she repeated. "Could you please check it out?"

"Okay, okay." He slid from the tent and stood up. Stretched. His back crackled like bubble wrap. And he yawned ferociously.

He leaned back down and looked into the tent. "You coming?" he asked.

"No. I'm staying here. You go check it out." She scooted a little further back into the tent. Away from the door.

"I'll check it out."

He stepped away from the tent and walked to the other side of their camp. It was an adorable little camp. Even the ring of rocks around the firepit was so picturesque it could have been an oil painting.

Eddie stepped around the pit and to the edge of the clearing.

He listened.

He heard trees in the wind and birds in the sky. He heard a rustling beyond the trees, out of his sight.

"Anybody out there?" he called out.

He counted to five.

"We have beer."

Nobody refused beer.

The rustling stopped.

Eddie strained his ears more and then gave up.

He turned back to the tent.

"Kate, it was probably a squirrel," he said. "This place is loaded with squirrels. And they sound like a person if they scream. I've heard it before."

He knelt and pulled aside the tent flap.

"You should come out and..."

The words died in his mouth.

Kate lay on her back, the great shaggy head buried in her torso shoving her back and forth as it fed. Her eyes were open and sightless, her skin curling and darkening.

The thing raised its head from the ruin that was her body, still chewing, and growled at him.

Eddie pulled back, but then something dark and gray struck him from the side. He fell against his face, never seeing what it was that ripped through his skin and spilled his blood and bones and meat out onto the forest floor. The teeth burned as they tore into him, and then the burning slowed and then Tony let himself go and he was no more.

Erin Makes Her Point

She wasn't technically an anarchist. Erin knew that. But it was entertaining to read *The Laws of the Jungle* anyway. She'd read it twice before. Now it was something she did for fun and to be able to share during quotable family moments.

Meredith was tossing a few dinner supplies into a box.

Then she stopped and stared at Erin.

Erin didn't have to look to know Meredith was staring at her. Meredith had an audible way of staring that Erin had come to know after many years of being on the downstream side of it.

It was a competition. Meredith would stare, hoping to use her brain powers to force Erin to acknowledge her. Erin, on the other hand, was tasked to ignore the stare, forcing Meredith to speak and thus acknowledge that she didn't actually have brain powers. The flaw in the competition was that Erin could compete without ever doing something and Meredith's brain powers required exertion. Meredith always lost.

"You going to help at all?" she asked.

Two seconds later – precisely enough to maximize annoyance – Erin looked at her sister.

"If I don't help," she said, "I'll be fed a nice dinner around a campfire. If I help, I'll be fed a nice dinner around a campfire and I'll be tired."

Meredith shook her head. "That's pretty selfish."

"You say selfish – I say pragmatic."

"Wouldn't it be more pragmatic, then, if you stayed home?"

"I suppose it would. I look forward to having the choice."

"Right, like when you move out?" Meredith set the box on the edge of the table.

"You're part of a family, Erin. Do you understand what that means? That means you're going to have to get used to participating in things."

"I think after seventeen years as a part of a family, I *am* used to it," replied Erin. "In fact, I'm more used to it than I think you are used to me not being comfortable with it. Why does it bother you that I don't like to be a part of a family that does family things and runs all over the countryside and toasts marshmallows and joins the PTA?"

"I have a problem with it because you're not interacting. You should be interacting."

"I am interacting. I'm interacting with you, right now. Is that not quality time? Are we not bonding in that special sisterly way? I paid for bonding."

"You can't go camping and then decide—"

"I'm not going camping. I'm along for the ride. I wanted to stay home. I would have preferred staying home. I have a ton of things I'd like to do at home, and I'm old enough to take care of a house for three days. Instead, I'm out here. Camping. I have Mom and Dad in my face and now I have you in my face. That's a lot of interacting. I don't think I like this interacting thing very much."

Meredith picked up the box and opened the RV door.

"Everybody needs somebody, Erin. Even you. You need somebody."

"Maybe *you're* not the somebody I need," said Erin. "You ever think of that?

"Maybe I *am* the somebody you need. *You* ever think of that?"

She stepped down and out onto the grass, but poked her head in. "Come on out when you're ready to join the human race."

She pushed the door shut behind her.

Erin stared at the door for a few seconds, then reached down and pulled up her pant leg. Strapped to her ankle was a throwing knife. She never felt the need for a throwing knife, but her friend Cole gave it to her, and it felt kind of bad-ass to strap it on. Besides, out in the woods, you never know, right? Might have to cut rope. Or clean a fish.

But this wasn't cutting a rope.

She drew the knife and tossed it in her hand, balancing it. She had practiced this part a lot.

She threw it across the room and it slammed into the cork organizer board next to the door. Right next to other puncture marks.

"Bitch."

The door opened. Meredith pushed her head back in. She looked at the knife coolly and then back at Erin.

"I'm about one 'fuck you' away from telling Mom and Dad where those holes are coming from," she said. "Don't push me."

"Meredith? I forgot to tell you something earlier."

The older sister raised one eyebrow in question.

"Fuck you. There. Tension broken."

Meredith stared.

"You draw that knife again and there's going to be some hurting, Little Sister, and it's not going to be me. *Capice?*"

She slammed the door shut.

Erin jumped out of the bunk and stepped to the door. Yanked the knife back out of the wall and sheathed it.

For a few seconds, she thought about going outside, and then changed her mind and locked the door.

"I hate you," she muttered.

She jumped back into the bed, facedown, and covered her head.

The Solution To A Family Problem

Burke was a good man. Sue loved him deeply. But he could be clueless. Not his fault, but worth keeping track of when things got dicey.

Helping him raise the shade structure helped her settle her mind. Physically engaged in building something, he was less likely to try and help out. His helping out tended to make things worse.

But even now, it might not be enough.

"The cord's too short," he muttered. He rarely muttered. Between wrestling the RV into the woods and the tension between the girls, he was running more ragged than she'd seen him run in a long time.

"Here," she said, and spooled more rope along the framework. "I have plenty on my side."

He yanked it over.

"Burke…" she said.

He glared at her, then back at the knot he was tying.

"I can't decide," he said. He yanked another loop on the knot. "I'm tempted to kill them both, frankly."

She nodded.

What she wanted to say was "Hon, you've got two daughters who are both on the rising wave of the puberty tsunami. Nothing they say or do is going to make any sense to you and getting between them will be like jumping into a chainsaw fight with nothing on but a g-string," but it came out "They're growing up."

He laughed bitterly.

"As I recall, you had similar problems with your brothers growing up," she said.

"Sure, yeah, once, but we settled it. After we settled it, it didn't keep happening and happening."

"Sometimes it takes more than once," she said. "With girls, there are complicating factors, too."

Ugh – she hated trying to explain this. Burke was a sweetie, but he knew nothing about how women worked. She did not enjoy the thought of trying to explain it to him.

Fortunately – or not – she was saved as Meredith stomped over, carrying the dinner supplies. Her face was a dark cloud.

Sue sighed. The next half hour was going to be difficult. Even more so than expected.

She touched Burke's arm. "Hon, could you go make sure the cooler's unpacked?" she asked.

At her touch, Burke looked up, confused. Then he saw Meredith. Looked back at Sue.

"Yeah," he said.

Helpful Dad needed to become absent.

At home, Helpful Dad went into the basement and worked on projects that required loud power tools. In this case, though, Helpful Dad was out in the woods. No power tools and nothing to drown out the noise.

"I'll check the cooler," he said. The cooler was beside the RV. He planned to check the cooler, but it wasn't a large cooler and the checking was symbolic anyway. It would take about ninety seconds. After that, he planned to walk down the road for ten minutes. Maybe fifteen. Then have a smoke. Then walk back. He didn't smoke much, but when the girls fought, it sometimes was necessary, although loud power tools produced better results.

He stepped away as quickly as he could without looking like he was in a hurry.

Sue smiled at him. Her husband often meant well, but sometimes missed his cues. In this case, he hadn't, and she was grateful.

She turned as Meredith approached and modulated her voice toward casualness.

"Honey, can you help me with these cords?"

Meredith set down the box and stepped over, pulling cords taut and letting her mother tie off the ends.

Sue worked slowly, waiting until Meredith spoke first.

"Mom, why did we bring Erin?"

"We're a family. It's important to me. To us."

"We must be a family of masochists."

Sue nodded, giving a little time to her response. Calm and quiet and stable. That was how her therapist described this approach. It usually worked.

"Meredith, your sister's—"

"—a sociopath. That's what she is."

Sue stopped tying knots and stared Meredith down. On the inside, finding herself unreasonably angry at her daughter, and unreasonably angry at her other daughter and then unreasonably angry at herself for trying to make them all get along when it was such a horrible idea.

But calm and quiet and stable was running the final output.

Meredith looked away first.

"She's gonna end up living in the woods like the crazy people. Living in the woods and eating squirrels and writing crazy letters and blowing stuff up."

Sue returned to her work, still a carefully measured pace. "She's your sister, and that's not a very nice thing to say."

"Maybe not, but it's true. She hates me. She hates us. Did you know she threw a knife at me?"

"A knife?"

"Ask her."

"I expect I will. What did you do?"

"I didn't do anything."

"I mean, afterwards. What did you do afterwards?"

"I came here."

"To talk to me?"

"Well, yeah. And to bring this stuff over."

Sue nodded.

"I can understand wanting some space," she said. "I can understand each of you wanting some space. *Each of you.*"

Meredith started emptying out the box onto the picnic table.

"I just wish she wouldn't be such a—"

"*Meredith!*" No, no, remain calm. She tried. She tried hard. "Not everyone can be perfect."

As soon as she said it, she recognized her own sarcasm slipping in. Not good. Each of the girls offered their own special challenges, and Sue knew to walk carefully when they battled. She couldn't afford to take sides. But that didn't mean she wasn't aware of the flaws of each side.

Meredith looked up at the sarcasm and for a second, there was a flash of defensive fury in her yes.

I better get used to that if I keep talking without thinking, Sue thought.

She clamped her calm face on. "We all struggle with things," she said. *God, that was lame. Why not break open a fortune cookie and read directly from it?*

The bushes rustled.

They both looked over.

The thing stepped out of the flat green, into the edge of the clearing and shook itself.

Sue was puzzled. At first, she thought it was a dog. A big dog. Then she thought it was a wolf. A big wolf. Its fur was streaked white across its head. *Did wolves have streaks?* she wondered.

The first flush of worry touched her. She could hear it whooshing inside her ear like a cold tide.

Then another one stepped out of the brush, next to it.

"Mom...?"

Sue tried to shush her daughter.

A third and fourth creature came out. The first one's face was streaked with gray and black and white. The others were ordinary colors. Gray, brown, black.

They were huge.

"Holy shit, is that a wolf?"

The bigger one looked at the sound. Its eyes flashed like reflections, even in the sunlight.

Sue whispered "Meredith. Meredith, you should... you should go. Back to the car."

Meredith didn't move.

The big wolf raised itself on its hind legs. Six, maybe seven feet.

The others coiled around it.

All eyes were on Sue and Meredith.

"Dad?" called out Meredith, but her voice wavered.

"Burke?" Sue called out. "*Burke!*" she shouted.

She heard a sound that might have been his voice from behind the RV. She couldn't be sure, though, because of the thunder. No wait, it wasn't thunder.

It was growling.

In a single bound, the big one leaped, and the others were right behind it.

Sue screamed. At least she thought she screamed. It might have been Meredith screaming, too.

The Iron Fails

Burke wasn't sure what he'd heard until he heard the screaming.

The cigarette dropped from his mouth and he scrambled back around the RV.

For a second, he watched. He couldn't not watch.

Then, in his mind, the red came. It wasn't anger, it wasn't revenge, it was just red.

The crowbar lay on the ground, near the front wheel of the RV. He bent and his hand picked it up. His mind had nothing to do with this action.

Nor did his mind have anything to do with the scream coming from his throat. Or the running. Or the raising of the crowbar and the swinging of it against the skull of the first creature he came to.

In that respect, the red offered no help to him.

In another respect, it did, however. It prevented him from feeling the wall of teeth and claw that crashed against him in return. It prevented him from feeling his body torn open. It prevented him from feeling the flood of something alien rushing into his flesh from the ragged hole where his throat and chest used to be.

Once he was safely past caring, it finally let him go.

The Lucky Couple

"A toast!" Ray stood and raised his glass.

"Dude, c'mon, you're already drunk," hissed Matt.

Fact was, both of them were lit like trees at Christmas.

Ray leaned down at Matt and whispered "I know, but fuck it – it's a wedding. Where else you gonna toast anything?"

That is to say, he thought he whispered.

The room quieted down.

Emboldened, Ray pressed on.

"I want to toast the lucky couple," he said. He turned to make sure he had everyone's attention. The church's social room was far larger than it needed to be for the number of people who lived in Hatchet Valley, but today it was packed with hundreds of sweating guests.

Maybe two hundred, but Ray couldn't always tell if he was seeing that many people for real, or seeing them through gin-tainted eyes.

He wobbled a little.

"Lisa. Craig. Goddammit, I've known you two since you were babies. *Babies!*"

The new bride and groom grinned. Ray wasn't the only toasted person in the room.

"And I have never ever known any two people I thought were better made for each other."

Nervously, he sipped his drink. Gulped. Just as everyone else was about to follow suit, he continued.

"I'm not going to tell any stories, because you both know I have the dirt on either of you. But what I will say is that I love you both like a brother. And, uh, a sister. And if you ever need anything – ever – anything at all – and you *don't* ask for it, I will be deeply and permanently offended."

He stared at his glass a moment.

"And then I might spill. So let that be a warning to you!"

This time, he raised his glass and drained it and everyone else who could did the same thing.

With his head still tilted, hoping to get the last few drops of whatever was in there to drip into his mouth, Ray glanced out the window.

His head rolled back to something almost normal for a human being.

He squinted to see better, but again, there was that problem with the doubling vision he'd been wrestling with.

"Hey," he said. "Hey everybody. Check it out!"

He pointed through the window, but his arm wobbled as much as the rest of his body.

"Check out all the dogs!"

At that moment, the front door, opened to let the late summer heat drift out, darkened.

Great gray things leaped in.

Eight seconds later the first person screamed.

Sundown

The wolves of Hatchet Valley howled as the sun dipped below the edges of the mountains. This they did every night, calling to each other, marking out their territories, and reminding the few humans nearby that they were still there.

For a few minutes, that was the only sound in the darkness.

Then a different howling came. A howl that came from no wolf's throat. It was a deeper reverberating rumbling howl. It wasn't a calling out, or a marking of territory.

It was a warning.

Others of its kind answered and the night shook in fear, as these howls overcame the wolf howls.

Death had arrived in Hatchet Valley.

Mark Catches Up

Mark ran, panting and crazy. The air pounded in and out of his lungs, but it seemed to do no good and his entire chest felt like it was on fire. Still, he kept running. It's not as if he had a choice.

He wished he had better shoes. Of all the things to wish for, the only thing his brain could make sense of was that he wished he'd had better shoes. You wear nice shoes to a wedding. Not tennis shoes. Not hiking boots. He needed those kinds of shoes. Instead, he had dress shoes. Ill-fitting rental dress shoes.

He was not going to get his deposit back on the tux, either. The mud and blood and tearing had seen to that.

Like Shadows

They sped through the dark under the trees.

When they needed speed, they went on all fours. When they needed height, they rose on two paws.

They were hungry and panting as much as their quarry, but they didn't give up.

Every once in a while, one would stop, throw back its head and howl. Then the others would stop and respond.

They didn't know why they did it, they just did. It was part of them.

They would hear other cries, too, from other parts of the valley.

Their numbers grew.

A Family Reunion

Deedee leaned against the tree, panting. The ground was rough– even in the small clearing – and in the dark she knew the woods were going to become impassable. If she kept running like she had been, she was going to break her neck.

And not only *her* neck.

She looked down in her arm.

Sean wasn't crying, thank God, but he was awake and had that terror-face she had come to learn often precluded crying.

She petted him and sang a soft tuneless tune.

He calmed down. Not as much as she would have liked, but going from Red Alert to Yellow Alert under the circumstances was a huge improvement.

Slowly her breath came back, but her chest hurt and her throat was raw. Sweat glued her dress to her skin. It had been her favorite dress. Her *only* dress. She didn't normally do dresses, but a wedding was a special occasion. Everyone else she knew tended to wear boy clothes, even to weddings, but when she wanted to class the place up a bit, she wore a dress.

She had exactly one dress.

Which was pretty fucking ruined right about now.

Brush and branches had torn it in many places. Mud, sap, dirt, and blood streaked and stained the satin.

She shook her head and tried not to think of the blood, but that was like trying to not think of the cheese when you wanted nachos. It was all she *could* think about. *So much blood!*

Sean wiggled a little bit and she shifted him to the other arm. He settled in and his eyes almost closed.

Then she heard it. Something moved through the brush. Something big was coming.

46

She felt her body flood with the panic chemicals, and then a hedge opened and Mark stumbled out into the little clearing.

"Jesus, Mark!"

He looked up, as startled to see her as she was him. He stumbled over. Crashed over, more like it. He was noisy.

He looked like hell. Sweat, dirt, and sap streaked his torn tux.

And blood. She could tell, even in the dim light, that he had been splashed with it. More than she had. Well, she wasn't going to feel guilty about that – he was the man and it was his job to defend his family.

"You scared the shit out of me!" she hissed at him.

He leaned against the tree, catching his breath.

"Where's Tony?" she asked.

He shook his head. His mouth hung open as he panted. He was starting to calm down, but he was still noisy.

"Shit," she muttered.

"Why did you run off?" he asked.

She looked at him. Mark often missed things, but this...?

"They broke into the car, right?"

He nodded.

"Everybody's dead, right?"

He nodded, but he also glared at her in the nod.

"And you know that was the tip of the iceberg, right? They came out of the chapel when we arrived. So they had already been in there. You know that, right?"

He nodded again, straightening up.

"That's why I ran. So I could end up at least here, instead of there."

"But you left Mark? Jesus Christ, Deedee, you left Mark in the car!"

"He could come with me. He didn't. He stayed."

"He was my *brother*. Of course he stayed. He was waiting for me. You couldn't even fucking respect *that?!* He's dead!"

"And we're not," she shot back. "So before you pull your asshole inside out and throw it at me, remember that. I'm still alive, you're still alive, and Sean's still alive. So, yeah, Mark stayed behind, and that was his call, and I'm sorry, but we're alive. He's not. The voting period has closed."

Mark stared at her, panting.

She knew she had won this one. There was no problem invoking Sean couldn't solve. Mark might be a shitbag (or "a bad choice," as her mother suggested not-so-delicately), but he would fall in line if his son was threatened.

God, men were predictable.

In the distance, she heard a deep throaty howl. Her head jerked in that direction and she held her breath, listening. Mark did, too.

He turned to look at her and she looked back.

"You bring the gun?" she asked.

"What gun?"

"The gun in your brother's glovebox."

"He had a gun in his glovebox? How did you know?"

"When we stopped at the gas station, he made me write down his gas and stuff. That's when I saw it."

"Huh. I never knew."

"He's your brother."

He shook his head. "Jesus, shut up for a minute, okay? We gotta think of a way out of this."

"So I take it you left it in the glovebox."

"Yeah. Okay, yeah, I left it in the glovebox. I had no idea he had a gun, so it didn't occur to me to look for it. Besides, I didn't want to go back into the car. They were already around it. I ran."

She nodded. "Okay. So long as, you know, it's somewhere safe."

There was a moment. A moment when he looked into her eyes and she almost saw the old fire in him, the thing that lit him up when he was younger. For the smallest moment, she thought maybe she had gone too far, that she had pushed too much. But then the fire went out and he backed down. Of course.

"We need to keep moving," she said. "We need to find either something they can't cross, a stream or something, or maybe some shelter. Anything."

"Deedee?"

"We can't make a stand without weapons, but maybe we can hide ourselves, or hide ourselves in a place they can't get to. Maybe climb a tree or something."

"Deedee!"

She looked at him. "What?" she asked. Couldn't he see she was trying to figure a way out of this mess?

Now that she thought of it, she *had* been in the clear, until Mark's loudness and noisiness and gasping led those things right to them. She hadn't heard howls until he had shown up.

On cue, another howl, this one closer.

He pointed over her shoulder with his chin. "Why don't we call for help?" he asked.

She turned around and gasped. Through a break in the trees, she saw square lights. Windows! A cabin! And it looked close enough to run to.

She switched Sean to her other arm.

"Oh look honey," she said to him. "Daddy found someone else to help."

"Why do you do that?" he asked. "He doesn't need that shit."

"Neither do I," she said, and turned toward the cabin. "If you're coming, then now's a good time."

Together, they ran through the last of the underbrush and toward the cabin.

Underground Might Have Been Better

The five men ran in loose formation, their backpacks and gear clanking and rattling like an organic locomotive.

Jim was trying to not panic. Trying hard. This was supposed to be a fun afternoon, a fun adventure, a little exploring.

When they heard the first wolf, it was as they had resurfaced. At first, it was novel. Wolves. They knew wolves wouldn't attack a party of grown men.

Then the first wave hit. Toby and Joe went down, covered in fur and fury and claws and teeth.

There had been a few seconds of shock and then the shooting started.

Jim remembered that exact moment. He saw Brass swing his backpack around and draw a pistol from it in one motion, but before he fired, another gun barked. Apparently, Tom was carrying as well.

In a matter of seconds, three monsters lay dead. Next to the corpses of two men.

Then the other howling had started, from at least three different positions, and they all decided simultaneously that discretion was the better part of remaining alive.

Now it was closing time.

Jim was in decent shape, but panting hard as he ran. He could see Tom's long legs eating the ground. Brass trundled along, too, given than he was short. He didn't have the long legs, but it was obvious he had plenty of strength to spare.

Walt and John, however, were not. Neither of the twins were in terrific physical shape. Walt stumbled in the crazy desperate way a man stumbles when he's already fired off his auxiliary jets and even they're running out of fuel. Had John not been nearing his limit, he would be helping Walt, but for now, it was all he could do to keep up the pace. But then John would stumble and Walt would pick him up and drag him a few feet – enough to continue running again.

Brass turned to the rear and took a firing stance as they passed. Twice, his gun kicked and twice there was a howling yip from the mass of growling beasts chasing them.

John tripped, but Brass appeared behind him, arm around the other man's side, and pulling him upright.

"C'mon, c'mon, c'mon," he yelled. "You can do it!"

Somehow, John found a little more fuel and his legs picked up the pace.

All five of them topped off their speed.

"How far to the cars?" he asked of no one in particular. Maybe the air.

"About a quarter mile," puffed Brass.

"Shit! We're not going to make it," shouted Tom. "Not like this. Not with them so close."

He swung around and fired as the other men passed. Once.

A howling scream followed the report, then Tom returned to his ground-eating run.

She Discovers Her Limitations

The gunshots were getting closer. Erin heard the last three and they didn't sound far away at all. For a moment, she worried about stray bullets hitting her. It would suck to get this far and then get nailed by some asshole's stray bullet. Would she even notice?

But no, it looked far more likely werewolves would eat her.

Which had not been on her plans that day. Not at all.

She found a game trail, which made things much better for her. She could run flat out and not trip over a root or a rock. She was surprised that they couldn't run as fast as she expected wolves to run. Then she was thrilled. Then she discovered that they could still run fast, and she was less than thrilled.

She managed a small gain, but they were behind her and she knew it. She could hear them crashing through the brush.

This was not going to work. This was not going to solve the don't-get-eaten problem. She needed to solve *that* problem, and it was clear that the running plan was not a viable long-term solution. She was not built for running. She was built for reading. Not even youthful exuberance was enough to keep her full of breath and energy. She was petering out fast.

She cast desperate eyes around, but there was nothing useful she could find. Not even a stick to use as a weapon. Although, given that these things stood about twice as tall as she did, she couldn't imagine facing them down with a stick.

Maybe a tank. That would work. She could call the tank "stick" to make it authentic.

Then she spotted the tree.

It was a big red oak. All the other trees were evergreen trees, so they were leafy pillars, but the oak had branches. Low branches she could reach.

She didn't have a lot of time, but she did have enough extra energy that she pushed herself to a sprint and angled behind the oak.

The Gray Tide

The wolves flowed past like a gray tide of fur, each one panting and snarling, sometimes snapping at each other, but always advancing.

They knew that there was a running thing ahead of them, and that they would catch it. They knew it was a matter of time.

They didn't know this with any sort of intellectual precision. They knew this because that was the way of things with prey.

Each one trusted the ones ahead to find the running thing. None thought that there might be any reason to stop.

The tide passed, with one straggler.

She Discovers One of Their Limitations

Fifteen feet off the ground, Erin hung on a branch of the oak, clinging upside down to it like a baby monkey.

She heard the tide arrive, heard the howls and the snapping of teeth. She heard the slapping of their paws against the packed trail ground.

She closed her eyes and willed herself invisible. She was nothing. She was a bump on the tree, a piece of wood. She was nothing that interested them. She held her breath.

The wave passed.

She exhaled across a count of ten, and as quiet as she could, sucked in another breath. Her chest was on fire, but she wasn't going to let gasping spoil her hideout.

After four deep and quiet breaths, the fire calmed down and she was back to trying to not pant.

For another few minutes she hung to the tree, catching her breath. Regrouping.

Once she'd collected herself, she listened. The chase had moved on further down the trail. She heard no sounds below.

One howl froze her, but it was distant.

She pulled herself onto the branch, and slid down toward the trunk.

She was closer to the ground than she realized.

She smiled in the dark. "You guys can't smell for shit," she whispered. She already knew that they weren't ordinary wolves, but this was a realization that mattered. This realization was going into the back pocket for later.

Quietly, she shinnied down the trunk. Hung the last few feet, and then dropped to the ground.

Still no response from around her.

"You're not very good hunters." she whispered. She glanced up and down the game trail, and her eyes stopped on a distant glow. She squinted and saw windows lit in a cabin. She figured the distance between her and the cabin. Not so good. It was further down the game trail, but also in the bottom of the valley, and that was not going to make it easy for her if those wolf-things showed up.

On the other hand, if they were shitty hunters, she could be quiet when needed. That was one of those capabilities skilled readers perform without even thinking.

She headed toward the lights, as the howling returned.

Family Has Limits, Too

The lights were on, but there was no other sign of life. No fire in the fireplace, no smoke from the chimney, no sounds of a happy family laughing away the evening's chill.

Deedee stumbled onto the wooden porch. "Hello? Is anybody home?"

Mark followed, and went straight for the door. He knocked loud enough to hurt his knuckles, but at this point he didn't care.

"Hello?" he called out. He knocked again.

"No one's home," said Deedee. "Or they're already dead. Like at the church."

"No, no, I saw a light. Someone's home."

He knocked a third time.

"Hey, open up. I know you're in there, we can see the light."

It couldn't be empty, someone turned the lights on after it got dark, and dark was only a few minutes ago. So someone was in there. But maybe she was right. Maybe they had already been killed. Maybe the house was filled with more of those things. Maybe after all this, they were going to force a door open and then be torn apart.

Then he heard movement inside. Something sliding or shuffling. Shuffling. He was sure of it!

He knocked again.

"Can you hear me? Hello? We need inside!"

An old man's voice came through the door.

"Go away," he said.

Mark and Deedee looked at each other, then back at the door.

"You gotta let us in," she said.

"And I said go away," repeated the old man. "I'm pretty sure I said it right, too. Go away."

Mark tried the knob, and instantly felt both foolish and horrible. He felt foolish because, of course it was locked. He felt horrible because if it hadn't been locked, he would have pushed right in. And that would have been invasive. He didn't want to be invasive.

Except that he didn't want to be eaten by wolves, either, so that would have been an easy decision to make.

A howl broke the night. Still a ways off, but it reminded Mark that there was a time for respecting the property rights of others, and then there was a time for not getting eaten. This was the latter.

He banged on the door.

"C'mon, this is *serious*! Do you know what's out here?"

"We have a baby," offered Deedee. "He needs your protection!"

There was no response from the other side of the door.

Mark stared at Deedee, his mind putting together the pieces. Seeing her do it to someone else made it clear to him.

"You're using him," he whispered.

"If it works, it works," she whispered back, glaring at him.

The door unlatched and opened a crack.

A shotgun poked out, and behind it, Mark saw gray frizzled hair and crazy eyes.

"Don't bullshit me," the old man growled.

Deedee stepped into view, holding Sean. "See," she said. "We need in, please. We'll be good."

The old man looked back at Mark.

"Just the three of you?" he asked. "Just you and her and the baby?"

"Just us," Mark said. "Just the three of us. No one else. We'll be quiet, we won't cause any trouble."

Another howl rang out, closer.

"Please," pleaded Deedee.

Mark shifted on his feet. He felt so exposed out here. "C'mon," he said. He tried to say it simply, but it sounded more like a whine when it came out. "You can't leave us to fend for ourselves out here. You can't leave a baby out here with those things loose in—"

"Hey!" the old man barked. He opened the door a little more. "Shut up and get in here."

They didn't need a second invitation.

Jake Sets Some Ground Rules

The door was thick and solid. Mark was glad to see that.

The old man let them pass, then closed the door, pushing it hard until it latched. He threw the bolt. The big impressive black iron bolt.

Mark took in the cabin interior. Not all of it, but the basic bits. Homey, small, and made of actual logs and solid wood instead of having a log-looking exterior. Pictures showed an older couple, and all the pictures were happy pictures. The place smelled of woodsmoke and antiques and clean simple living.

The windows, however, had been boarded up, and by the looks of it, the old man was in the middle of adding reinforcements.

So he *did* know what was going on out there!

Mark turned to him and extended a hand. "Thanks for letting us—"

Mark wasn't sure what had slugged him in the side of the head, but it was fast and it was hard. His ear rang and his head wobbled and there was a whooshing sound in his brain.

He felt himself shoved hard against the wall and someone pressing against him.

Holy crap, I let an old guy get the drop on me! he thought.

A cold metal thing jabbed him under the chin and pushed up. He didn't have to guess – he knew it was the shotgun. The old man held Mark against the wall with one arm across his chest and held the shotgun halfway through his throat.

"Mark!" Deedee called out.

"Shut up, both of you," the old man said. "Shut up and listen."

In the voice, Mark heard something. Something desperate or afraid or broken or maybe just plain crazy. He couldn't decide which. He held his hands up a little, bending at the elbows.

"It's cool," he tried to say around the shotgun, but it came out like a gargle.

The old man leaned in close.

"No," he growled. "It is not cool. Not by any stretch of the imagination is it cool. You are in my home. If you want to be in my home, then you had best get the rules down. Rule Number One, you have no right to be here. You're here because I am *letting* you stay and I can kick your ass out at any time. You, your woman, *and* your baby."

"We were just—" Deedee started to say, but he interrupted her.

"Do you understand Rule Number One?"

Mark nodded.

"Good. Rule Number Two."

He turned and stared at Deedee.

"No one interrupts me. If you interrupt me, then you are outside. No discussion. No bullshit."

He turned back to Mark.

"That goes for both of you. Do you understand Rule Number Two?"

Mark nodded again. He was starting to regret finding the cabin.

"Rule Number Three is for you," said the old man, and he leaned close and put his lips to Mark's ears and whispered. "Rule Number Three is that if you *ever* try to manipulate me with guilt, or manipulate me by threatening a child again, I will personally blow your *fucking* head off."

He pulled back and looked into Mark's eyes. Whatever had been in his voice earlier, was completely one hundred percent behind Rule Number Three. Never touch a crazy person's buttons.

In a normal voice, he said "I think you understand Rule Number Three, don't you? You seem smart."

Mark nodded. *Jesus, this guy was a lunatic!*

He backed off and pulled the shotgun away from Mark's throat. Deedee rushed up and wrapped herself around him.

"Who are you?" the old man asked. Mark introduced himself, Deedee, and Sean.

"I'm Jake," the old man said. "And this is my place. You'll be fine here, I expect."

Mark hesitated a moment, then asked "Do you have a phone?"

"No phone."

"Maybe a car?" asked Deedee. "We could drive out of here – all of us."

"No car," said Jake.

Outside, a car horn honked. Three times.

"No car?" asked Mark.

Jake ran to the windows and peered out between the boards.

"What the hell are they *doing?!*" he asked.

Riding On Fumes

Rose's fingers were bone white on the steering wheel. She squinted through the blood smeared on the outside windshield of the Corolla. She'd tried using the windshield wipers ten minutes ago, but there was no fluid, and things got worse instead of better.

The Corolla lurched again.

"We're not gonna make it," warned Carter from the seat next to her. His head was turned around and he watched the road behind them like a hawk.

"We're gonna make it, baby."

She glanced at her husband. Even streaked with blood and sweat, and half-panicked, he was an angel. His eyes were sweet blue and his hair and beard were brown and gold. Anything she had to do to make it, she was going to do it.

Eyes back to the road ahead. The Corolla jerked again.

"We're cavitating," said Carter. "We're dry."

"Not yet. We're almost there."

"They're following us," he said. "They're going to catch up."

"Not before we get there."

"What if we get there and no one's home?" he asked.

"We always wanted a little cabin in the woods. And stop being such a Negative Nellie. It doesn't suit you."

She felt a touch on her cheek and looked over. His fingertips. He smiled at her.

"I love you, you know that, right?" he said.

"I told you we're gonna make it," she said. "Don't give up now."

The wagon jumped ahead as a pocket of gas made it into the line.

"They still behind us?"

Carter squinted into the growing darkness. "I saw one at least," he muttered. "But it's all in and out of the woods, so I don't know. Might be two. Maybe three."

"How close?" she asked.

"Real close," he replied. "How close to the cabin?"

"Real close," she answered.

Suddenly she had an idea. She hit the horn.

"What are you doing?" he asked.

She hit the horn again. "I don't want to wait on the porch," she said. "If they're that close, we will be running when we hit the ground. If there's someone in there, I want that door open."

She honked a third time.

The car lunged once more, and then the engine died.

Her foot slammed down on the clutch and they coasted.

"Shit!" said Carter.

"We'll make it. Grab the bag. Get ready."

She saw him pull the shoulder strap of the gear bag around his neck. He patted himself down and nodded. Put a hand on the door latch. "Ready when you are," he said.

Godammit, she loved a man who could be ready in two seconds to sprint out of a dead car and run from werewolves.

The car rolled to a stop.

"Come on!" Rose shouted as she kicked her door open.

She knew he was a few steps behind her as she crossed in front of the car. At least the ground under her feet wasn't treacherous.

She looked at the cabin.

Not as close as she would have liked. Not at all.

"Let's run this fucker down," she said, grabbed his hand, and lit out.

Sometimes it's an Easy Choice.

Place Your Bets

"You idiots," muttered Jake. "They're gonna tear you apart."

Mark and Deedee were also pressed to cracks in the wood, watching the car, and then watching the couple step from the car, and then watching them run.

Deedee straightened up. "We can't let them in," she announced.

"Deedee, what the hell?" asked Mark.

"We can't let them in. We'd be opening the door, endangering all of us here. We probably don't have enough room or supplies. Three's a crowd."

"Four," muttered Jake, never taking his eyes off the scene outside. "Still not used to the baby, huh?"

She looked down at Sean.

"That's not good," said Jake.

Mark turned back to the view. "Oh no!"

Outside, a huge gray shape jumped out from the shadows near the cabin, between the running couple and the front door.

"Your gal's right," said Jake. "We can't help 'em."

"Can't we do *anything?*" asked Mark.

"I only have so many shells. I can't be spending them on people who are helpless."

Never Judge A Book

It wasn't an impossible run, just a longer one than it should have been.

Carter saw the thing come out of the darkness. It rose between them and the cabin.

At that moment a Bad Fantasy entered his mind. The Bad Fantasy was that the cabin might not be empty, but instead filled with more of these wolf-things. All teeth and claws and well-sheltered hunger waiting for desperate passersby.

He skidded to a stop.

"Rose!"

He dropped to his knees and fingered the zipper on the bag. "If I can get the—"

"No time, baby," said Rose. She drew her revolver.

The thing leaped.

Her revolver split the air with a boom.

Two hundred pounds of shaggy no-longer-toothy hit the ground and lay still at their feet, its head flowered open by the Mag.

"You furry *fucker!*" she screamed. She kicked its neck.

She was the most dangerous, the most powerful, and the most beautiful woman Carter had ever seen. She was a goddess. A short, deadly, Irish goddess.

He leaped up, and pulled her onward toward the cabin.

A Cautious Meeting

"Son of a bitch!" cried Mark. "She nailed it!"

Jake pushed past him, beelining for the door.

"Wait, what are you doing?" asked Mark.

"Getting the door."

"But you said we weren't going to let them in."

"That was before I saw they weren't helpless."

Jake pulled back the bolt, flipped the latch, and yanked the door open. Raised his shotgun to cover the two incoming people.

"*Run!*" he yelled.

Feet pounded the dirt. Then the wooden porch. Then Carter and Rose tumbled through the door.

Jake slammed it shut behind them and threw the heavy bolt.

Outside, a frustrated howl split the air.

The newcomers panted their way to equilibrium. Outside, claws paced back and forth on the front porch. After a few minutes of frustrated whining, the sounds died out as the creature wandered off.

Mark watched it through a crack in the window boarding.

"It ran off," he whispered. Everyone released a breath. "It went into the trees, but I couldn't see it any further than that."

Jake eyed the new couple. The gal looked hard. Not brutal, but like someone who's seen more than she should see, and dealt with it. She sure as shit made short work of that critter without a moment's hesitation.

Her fella looked a little soft, though. Almost like a reformed hippie. Jake felt a pang of connection to that sensibility, but he split from that path many years ago, back when he saw the blood-soaked machinery of democracy and its effects on people. His years of peace and love were behind, stolen from the present. Those challenges left him feeling as hard and brittle as the woman across the entryway.

He nodded at her.

"That was a nice shot, Red. Was that a lucky shot, or are you really that good?"

"My name's not Red," she said. "It's Rose." She holstered the revolver. "And it *was* a lucky shot. To be fair, however, *all* my shots are lucky shots."

Jake nodded again. A good attitude, too. Not cocky.

"Either of you hurt? Bitten? Scratched?"

They looked at each other, then back at him.

"No," said the man. "None of that. Scratched?"

Jake extended a hand and introduced himself. Carter swung his bag over his shoulder and shook it. "Carter Swan," he said.

Jake looked into the man's eyes and started to change his mind. There was something intense in those eyes. Something unpredictable. Something that hadn't been visible at first blush. Jake made a note of it.

Rose shook his hand, and confirmed what he thought – everything she did was deliberate.

He was glad they were here. But still, not sure.

"Why did you stop?" he asked.

"Out of gas," said Rose.

"We got lost. Turned around," said Carter. "We were hoping to make it to the other end of the road."

"There is no other end of the road in Hatchet Valley," said Jake. "Only one goddamn road and it ends at my place."

"We were visiting a friend," said Carter. "It got a little confusing at the end, there."

"Which friend?"

Carter and Rose exchanged a glance.

The Cougar

Three years ago, Jake and Lucy had been hiking one of the steeper trails. Nothing too treacherous, but rocky and inaccessible. They had paused for a while, tucking into a little scooped-out portion of the rock face. It was out of the wind, and they were also in love, so that all made sense at the time. The bright morning sun splashed across the path and they sat there, with no cares whatsoever, enjoying the spectacular view down into the valley.

Just then, a kitten stumbled into view. A cougar kitten. It walked and ran and tumbled its way down the path – the same path Jake and Lucy would have been walking up, had they not stopped. The kitten bumbled along, and as it went out of view, two more kittens rolled down, mock-fighting with each other. Back and forth they rolled, batting and snarling in the adorably ferocious way that big predatory cats can act when they are still small and harmless.

Then their mother came into view.

Jake and Lucy knew there were cougars in the valley, particularly up the slopes. But this wasn't an ordinary cougar. She was huge. Her paws alone were as wide as a grown man's head.

Jake and Lucy froze in place. There was nothing else to do.

The cougar moved with a deliberate grace, following her kittens.

Just as they thought she was going to pass, the cougar stopped, a few yards away. She raised her great head and her nostrils flared. Then she looked directly at them.

The cougar stared at them for almost ten seconds, but it seemed like a week. Maybe a month. No movement, no breathing. Her flat brown eyes looked them over, assessed them, and decided – thankfully – that they weren't posing enough of a threat to the kittens.

Then the cougar turned and continued down the trail.

They held their breath for at least another thirty seconds after she left.

Suddenly Thick

Jake remembered how it felt to have that big cat watching, assessing, so assured of its power that it never once felt the need to make a threatening gesture. He knew what it meant to miss through sheer luck something deadly.

This was exactly what the room around him felt like.

Jake was not used to feeling this in his own house.

Rose spoke in an even tone. "Carter, baby, what was your friend's name?"

"Jefferson. Jefferson Greene," replied Carter. His voice was also flat. Careful.

Jake was worried. A little. Somehow in a way he never noticed, Rose's hand had slipped behind her back. As if it belonged there.

But still, this was his house. That mattered. Anyone could offer a name.

"You know Caterpillar Greene?" he asked. He'd been played before.

"Not well enough to know a nickname," answered Carter.

Shit, they knew this game. Not a surprise, considering the look of them. Jake thought about it a second, but realized he needed people. Not just anybody, but the right kind of people. This kind of people. The kind of people who could shoot things such that the things didn't get back up afterward.

He relaxed a little.

"How's Jeff doing?" he asked.

"He's dead," said Carter.

"They got to him. We saw it," said Rose.

"Jesus. They made it to *his* place?"

Rose nodded. He could see her relax a little, and the room tension dropped.

"Almost got to us, too," said Carter. "Barely made it back to the car."

Jake turned to him. "But out of gas," he said.

Rose shrugged. Jake was relieved that he could see her hands again.

"I've got gas here," he said. "But someone's gotta run it out to your car. I don't know if that's such a good idea."

Deedee stepped up. "Mark'll do it!"

"Buh— *what?!*" Mark nearly spit.

"Sure, you were a runner."

Mark shook his head. "In high school! That was almost twenty years ago."

Deedee pointed toward the door. "How hard can it be?"

"Are you kidding? I almost died out there and that was a little running through the woods. You don't stay being a runner unless you run all the time." Mark looked at her as if he couldn't believe this required an explanation.

Jake was starting to find both their voices more annoying than before.

Deedee stared her husband down. "Okay, great," she said. "Fine. Is there anything else I need to know?"

This confused Mark.

"What?"

"Because," she said. "I know my limitations. I know what I can and can't do. But apparently, I don't know *your* limitations. I was under the impression you had all this running experience. So, now I discover you don't."

"Deedee, no one can run like that. No one. And with those things out there, it would be suicide."

Deedee shrugged "How would I know," she said. "I'm not the athlete in the family."

Jake was still trying to parse this exchange. He shook his head. Mark caught his eye and shrugged, as if to say "Women – what can you do?"

No, no, Jake was not going to get caught in their whirlpool.

"I guess," said Deedee. "I'm going to have to raise two children instead of one."

"No," said Jake.

They both looked at him.

"I want you idiots out of here."

"What?" asked Deedee.

"Now. I want you out of my house. Both of you."

Mark started to speak "Wait a minute..."

"No. No 'wait-a-minute.' You two are nothing but crazy throwing crazy at crazy, and I'm not going to put up with it. So, I want you out of here."

Rose and Carter glanced at each other. Jake spotted that out of the corner of his eye, but wasn't going to deal with that right now. Right now it was time to clear the pipes.

He pulled the hammers back on the shotgun. In the silence, they double-clicked loud.

Deedee pleaded "You can't throw us out. Not out there. Not tonight."

"They'll kill us," said Mark.

"Not my problem," said Jake. "If I didn't want to conserve my own ammunition, I'd be likely to as well. I'm tired of hearing your voices. Now out!"

He pushed them toward the door.

They bumbled and fumbled like sheep that had already seen the ones in the front of the chute dying, but couldn't quite get the fact that they were in the same queue.

Deedee hid behind her husband. "Mark, do something," she said.

Mark stared at Jake. Jake stared back. Jake knew his type, though. He knew that Mark was one of those sorts of people who can be stared down, because they never learned they could run their own world. He knew it would be quick. He didn't even have to move. Mark would back down.

Mark backed down.

"Okay," he said, softly. "I get it. Your house."

He reached for the doorknob, resting a hand on it.

"Fine."

He turned it slowly, watching Jake.

There was no backing down on this one. Jake never moved.

Mark sighed.

"Okay," he said. "Okay, we'll go. But I want you to know this is your choice. You're sending us outside."

71

Jake's eyes narrowed. "You remember Rule Number Three?" he asked in a low voice.

Mark paled, then turned and opened the door.

At first, there was nothing, because people don't often look below their knees. It must have crawled onto the porch and been lying across the threshold.

When the door opened, however, the thing arched and stood on two legs.

The long claws at the ends of the hands waved like snakes about to strike.

Rose drew, but Jake knew he was in her way. She wouldn't shoot.

He already had his gun out and cocked, but that asshole and his wife were standing straight in the line of fire.

"*Out of the way!*" he shouted, although there was a small part of him that wanted to kick hard against them right at the same moment, shoving them out and onto the beast.

Deedee screamed and grabbed Mark.

Now they were an even more solid mass blocking the doorway, blocking anyone from shooting.

At that moment, there was a double report from outside. The creature's head and shoulder exploded and it flew sideways off the porch.

A New Company

It had been a remarkable shot, and Jim was impressed. Terrified, too, but impressed.

They had pulled up behind the other car as the front door opened and before he had a sense of what was going on, Tom and Brass had already leaped out of the car, guns drawn.

The thing on the porch was dropped within three seconds.

"C'mon guys, let's go!" he said to the twins.

The three of them tumbled out of the Suburban. Jim ran toward the cabin, but Walt and John stayed together.

"Jim," shouted Walt. "I don't know if this is a good idea. The car's steel. We're safe there."

Something huge leaped to the roof of the Suburban, something built of muscle and fur and teeth and claws.

It growled and jumped, pulling Walt and John to the ground.

There was one shriek, and then both men were torn open.

Jim stared. This made no sense. No sense at all.

Tom and Brass stepped to either side of him and fired.

The thing jumped at the impacts, and stood up. Its shoulder bled.

Its eyes flashed at them and it leaped.

There was a peculiar boom.

It dropped, its head gone.

Jim looked at it, then at Tom and Brass. They looked at each other and shrugged. All three looked back at the cabin.

On the porch, an old man knelt, his shotgun still aimed, smoke curling from the muzzle. Behind him a woman stood with a pistol as big as her head. Its muzzle also smoked.

The old man looked up from his aim.

"You better move it," he said. "They're still close."

They moved it.

An Exit Is Planned

The three men hit the porch running, but stopped at the door.

There's an order to certain social events. If giant wolflike monsters are attacking someone, and you're in range and have a decent chance at making the shot, it's okay to fire your weapon. People are okay with that. On the other hand, it's generally frowned upon to race to someone's front door with a weapon drawn. In this instance, then, there was a brief moment of confused social awkwardness. The lack of a clear "Come inside!" signal exacerbated that. Those who had been on the porch remained on the porch. The new people were now on the porch. There were no monsters, yet guns were drawn. Awkward indeed.

Carter assumed the pale one was the leader. If it could be said that they had a leader. There were three, and to Carter, they were the tall one, the stocky one, and the pink one that looked overwhelmed.

Then again, maybe they didn't have a leader.

Carter watched and waited for a cue from Jake.

Jim knew something had to happen. A frozen moment like this would not end well. Less so the longer it lasted. His brain sifted data, but it could not find any existing protocols for gun-laden face-offs on porches while surrounded by dead wolf-monsters.

So he fell back on the Universal Social greeting. A gift.

"We have a car. You guys need out of here?"

"Hell yeah!" said Carter. He turned to Jake. "Anything you need?"

"Nothing I can't come back for." Jake turned to Jim. "There's five of us plus a baby. That okay by you?"

"It's gotta be. Let's get the fuck out of here!"

He turned to the stocky guy. "Brass, can you get it started. Let's get the fuck out of here."

Just as they turned toward the car, there was an engine rev. Not an ordinary rev, but a crazy uncontrolled high-speed rev.

Damn, that was fast, Carter thought. Then his brain connected the sound to the time and fired off a cognitive warning shot. As he looked up, a green station wagon fishtailed into view down the road. Gravel sprayed out behind it.

Too fast was all he managed to think before the station wagon plowed into the back of the Suburban.

The Suburban took the hit like a paper bag, collapsing in the back and springing forward, smashing into Rose and Carter's Corolla. Meanwhile, the wagon vaulted ass end up, spinning around. Its momentum pushed it onto the Suburban, and when gravity finally caught up and yanked it back to Earth, it landed on top of the Corolla, facing backward. The Corolla's cabin was crushed and the station wagon tilted upward from the collapse, looking to all the world as if it were perhaps a station wagon-flavored rocket ship about to take off. Again.

"My truck," whispered Jim.

"My car," whispered Carter.

"Holy shit!" said Mark. "Did you see that? *Holy shit!*"

From inside the wagon, a groan answered.

Jim and Brass exchanged a glance, and then they both ran out to the wrecks.

Carter turned to Jake. "It always this busy?" he asked.

Some Parts May Be Damaged During Shipment

Jim hit the wagon first. The driver-side door was bent open, and he pulled it the rest of the way. A woman hung from the seatbelt, long blonde hair hanging in her face and the deflated airbag still splattered against her body.

She moaned again.

"You okay?" he asked. The question felt fatuous, but it was the first thing and the only thing he thought of. He felt around the seatbelt. Everything was jammed tight.

She moaned again, tried to speak.

"Hey, hey, I hear you. I hear you. You're okay. Can you hear me?"

She managed to speak, just above a whisper. "*Ach du scheisse...*"

Jim stopped. "Uh. I'm sorry. Do you speak English? We're friends." He hoped she understood "friends."

Brass came up behind Jim. He glanced across the wreck. "Toast," he observed. "We need to get her inside."

A howl split the air.

"We need to get her inside *soon*," corrected Brass.

"Where am I?" the woman whispered. She looked at them, tried to focus. Her hair was in the way.

Jim gently wiped her hair away from her face. "You've been in a crash," he said. "But you'll be fine. We gotta get you out of your car and inside. Can you move?"

She concentrated. "I can't feel my legs," she said. "I don't know what that means yet, but maybe not so bad."

Jim nodded. "Yeah, maybe not so bad. That's okay – we can help, but we have to get you out of the car."

He looked under the dashboard.

Carter ran up. "What's going on?" he asked. "She okay?" He looked at the woman. "You okay?"

She shrugged a little. "I'm still alive. That counts today, I think. But I can't move my legs."

"She's pinned," Jim told him. "If we can roll her to the left, I think we can get her clear."

Carter nodded. "Okay, let's do it. Who wants to push the dashboard up and who wants to roll?"

Brass stepped forward. "I'll push the dashboard."

"You got it. Uh, I'm Carter, by the way."

Jim nodded. "I'm Jim and this is Brass. C'mon, let's get her out of there."

"Okay. Uh, ma'am, is it okay if we roll you a little?"

She nodded. "My name's Claire. Please don't call me 'ma'am.' Just Claire."

"Claire, Carter and I are going to roll you and I think we can get you out."

"What can I do?"

"Just relax, I guess."

"Yeah, it might sting a little," said Carter. "You might have turned it or something."

They held her and she relaxed into his arms.

"Okay," said Jim. "Let's turn her this way..."

Brass pushed on the dashboard and it rose a few inches with a creaking rattle.

Claire hissed, and involuntarily rolled back.

"Oh jeez, sorry," said Jim.

"Maybe it's broken? It hurt," she said.

"Maybe. I don't know."

Jim looked under the dash. Brass came in closer. Jim pointed. "If you can get that one piece there to lift high enough, we might be able to pull her out without turning, but I'm afraid it might—"

"Hey!"

They both pulled their heads out from under the dash and looked toward the cabin. Jake was waving at them and pointing down the road.

Jim, Brass, and Carter all looked. There was movement.

Brass turned to Jim. "I'll do what I can, but now is the time."

Jim turned to Carter. "You ready?"

"What's happening?" asked Claire.

"We're out of time," said Jim.

Another howl, this one closer.

Claire's eyes opened wide. "Oh no," she whispered. "I thought they weren't real."

Carter touched her shoulder. "They're real and they're coming. I'm sorry, but we gotta get you inside where it's safe."

He looked at the wreckage of the dashboard.

"I think this is going to hurt a bit," he said.

She looked back at him and nodded. "I understand. Hurry, please. Hurry."

"Wait, wait!" said Jim. "Hey, can you undo your seatbelt?"

Claire blinked. Her right arm fell behind her seat and with a click, the belt slid free.

As she slipped away from the seat, Carter caught her. She gasped in pain again.

"I'm sorry," said Carter. "I know it hurts. I think it's going to hurt more than that. But we need to get you inside."

He turned to Jim and Brass. "Maybe the two of you together can move it more?"

The two men pushed. The dashboard moved and creaked.

"Come on," whispered Carter. He started pulling Claire free, but she barked a short scream. "I know, I know, it hurts like shit. I'm sorry. Hey guys, can you give us more room?"

Another howl. Closer.

"Carter!" That was Rose.

"Now, Carter, now. We can't lift any higher," said Jim.

Carter looked at Claire. "We can't do any better," he said, holding her. She nodded. Closed her eyes and started hyperventilating.

"Fuck it," said Carter. "Shove!"

Brass and Jim pushed. The dash raised another inch, but the car's frame blocked it after that. In that instant, Carter knew that no amount of force would raise the dashboard any higher. He also knew that it wasn't raised high enough. He also knew this was going to hurt. He also knew he was out of time.

Sometimes we know too much, he thought.

He pulled.

Claire screamed.

He pulled harder.

Her fingers dug into his bicep and her scream rang in his ears, and he pulled even harder.

You Can't Always Get What You Want.

"Shit," muttered Rose. "Shit, shit, shit."

"They ain't gonna make it," said Jake.

Rose knelt. Took aim with that great hand cannon she wore. "Shut up and aim," she muttered.

Jake raised the shotgun. Too far away, but he was going to try.

It's A Matter Of Rhythm

Carter heard Rose call out, but he couldn't hear what she said. He knew she wanted him back. Hell, he wanted to be back. The air felt nice and cool, but he knew it was in the open, and in the open were things that would kill him.

The woman – Claire – screamed as she dug her fingers into his arm. Shit, that hurt.

He pulled more, and she screamed louder.

At the end of her scream, he heard the deep guttural howl of those things.

That's when everything switched to beats. He felt it like a computer clock pulsing inside him, a heart-driven bass clef that made everything work in sync.

Heartbeat.

He knew what he had to do. He knew Claire must be pulled out, regardless of the state of her foot. He knew it was going to hurt. A lot. He knew she was going to scream. *What if I'm not strong enough? What I fall? What if we both fall and things got a lot worse?*

Heartbeat.

He looked into her eyes. Her face was pale. Her cheeks bright red. Her eyes wide and scared. Sweat bathed her. She was soaked in it. And she panted.

Heartbeat.

"I'm sorry," he said, and she closed her eyes. *How did she know,* he wondered? How could she not.

Heartbeat.

He braced his feet against the ground and swayed toward the car, holding Claire. This is so wrong. *This is going to be horrible.* He glanced once at the dashboard, at the leg disappearing under it, and the other two men pushing it up.

Heartbeat.

He jerked back from the car, rebounding against his sway and pulling her free. There was a sound. A loud triple crack. Claire's body locked around him like a clamp, and she screamed.

Footstep.

No, no, I can't fall! I braced myself! He felt the world sway, he felt the weight in his arms, he felt the woman convulse.

Footstep.

Somehow, his left foot made it underneath him. His right foot had already left the ground. I can do this, I can balance, I can hold her.

Footstep.

Both feet on the ground. Safe.

He looked at the other two men – *I did it, I have her!* – but they were gone. The scream stopped and Claire went limp.

Heartbeat.

The other two men were already a third of the way back to the cabin and running.

Run!

The sync wasn't right. He couldn't start running until something happened. Until the clock ticked.

Heartbeat.

His leg pushed against the ground, not at all under his own control, pushing him toward the cabin. Toward the crowd. Toward Rose.

Heartbeat.

Footpush.

I'm not going to make it. I can't believe I'm even trying. What was I thinking – I can't carry a full-grown woman. This is stupid. I don't even know if she's still alive.

Heartbeat.

Footpush.

I'm doing it, though. I'm doing it. I'm running and I'm carrying her. Jesus, I'm actually doing it!

Heartbeat.

Footpush.

C'mon, legs! More, more, more. Oh god, what if I tore her foot off? What if that was what I heard, her foot coming off? What if she's bleeding like crazy? What if she's dying? Dying as I carry her. What have I done?!

Heartbeat.

Footpush.

I can't look. I gotta keep running, gotta get her over there. We can help her inside, maybe use a tourniquet. Or maybe a belt. Or some rope. Whatever. Oh, I hope I don't have to go back and get her foot.

Heartbeat.

What is this? What's wrong with the ground? Is this a hill? Why am I at a tilt? Why am I—? Oh no, oh no, I can't fall now. I can't trip now. I'm so close!

Heartbeat.

I can't feel the ground. Where is the ground? Rose, Rose, I'm sorry, I can't feel the ground. I'm falling and I don't know where the ground is and this woman needed help and now I've fucked it all up and I'm sorry.

Heartbeat.

Arms around her. Sorry.

Uff! Wha—

The sky. That's the sky. I'm okay. I'm on my back. I'm okay!

Heartbeat.

Dark.

No, not dark. Shadow.

I see you. I see you, and how did you get so close? Teeth and ears and eyes. Golden eyes. I see you and there is no sky.

And now you are gone. Now you are neck. Only neck. And warm.

"Carter!"

Rose.

84

The Open Sky

Rose yanked the body off Carter. Curled beneath the headless thing was her husband, and curled inside his arms was the woman from the car.

For a fraction of a second, she thought she was too late. His eyes were cool and distant, staring unblinking into the sky.

"Carter!" She dropped to her knees and cupped his face. *Not now, not a good time, not ready to lose you, baby.*

He blinked, and then came back.

"Shit!"

"C'mon, c'mon!"

She pulled the pair of them up. Carter stumbled, but kept his balance, still holding the woman.

Jake's shotgun boomed.

Another wolf went down.

And then they were on the stairs and past the door.

Better Than Nothing

"Clear the couch! Clear the couch"

Carter ran, unconscious arms and legs dancing around him as he carried Claire. "Move the table!"

Mark swung around and pushed the coffee table away from the couch.

Carter dropped her into the couch and collapsed next to her, panting.

Another shotgun boom from the front door.

"Goddammit – they're everywhere!" the old man shouted.

Another boom.

The door slammed shut.

Carter steeled himself to look at her feet, to look at the bleeding raw stump where her foot used to be, to be ready to wrap off the spurting blood and—

—and it looked fine.

Maybe not fine. She lost a shoe. But she still had a foot. Scratches and scrapes, a little trickle of blood. And the ankle looked dark. That made sense.

He heaved a sigh – it was almost a laugh – of relief. She still had a foot!

"She gonna be okay?" Mark asked.

"I'm not a doctor," said Carter. "But she has her feet. See?"

It's The Quiet Ones

This was getting out of hand. Jake threw the locks on the door and turned for the living room. For a moment, he thought of leaving his shotgun next to the door, but then changed his mind. He wasn't afraid of any of these people, but things were way out of control and it was time to have his hands on something a little less dangerous than some asshole's neck.

The blonde was laid out on the couch. Red and her guy were kneeling beside her, and everybody else stood around looking like they wanted to be somewhere else.

He looked down at the unconscious woman's face. Yeah, unconscious. Not dead. That was good.

He looked at her foot. That ankle was gonna hurt.

"How's she doing?"

"She's breathing."

Carter. That's right, his name was Carter.

"She won't be walking any time soon."

Carter shook his head. "Yeah, dancing's right out, too. We need a doctor."

Jake shook his head. The nearest doctor he knew of was all the way at the other end of the valley, and that was not in a direction he wanted to go right now.

Jim spoke up. "Tom? Can you help?" He was looking toward the gaunt one that arrived with him.

Tom glared back. "I'm a vet."

"A vet's a doctor."

"I can't work on people, Jim."

"We need you."

"Hey, both of you!" Jake did not feel one bit like listening to this horseshit anymore. He nodded toward the one called Tom. "You're a vet?"

Tom nodded.

"Good. Dogs have legs and bones, too, so could you please just fucking check her?"

Is that supposed to be a withering kind of look you're giving me? thought Jake.

Tom knelt down and ran his fingers over the ankle. Pressing, tapping, turning it a little in each direction. His eyes were closed.

"Doesn't feel broken," he muttered.

"You're doing great, doc, keep at it."

He turned then to the corner of the room. The darker corner. The corner his eyes had brushed by as he came into the room. The corner where the thin girl crouched, watching everyone, not moving, half-hidden behind the side table.

He stared at her.

"So then, who the hell are you?"

Jake Finds One Possible Solution

Damn, he was attentive for an old guy. The instant he turned and looked straight at her, Erin knew there was no hiding. Everything was looking promising three minutes ago. The path was clear, the critters were distracted, and the cabin a good place to vanish into. Maybe a closet or an attic, or someplace safer than the open woods. Actually, any place would be safer.

And then everyone had rushed in, carrying the woman, and rushed around looking for doctors, and the only thing Erin could do to avoid being seen was to crouch low and stay still.

Which normally worked. Normally.

But she was caught and he was a smart one and this was one of those times when you have to hope it goes well.

Considering he already looked pissed, and that he carried a shotgun, that was a lot of hope.

Also, it didn't help that everyone was silent now, staring at her.

Sometimes when older people confront you, you can tell them some bullshit story, spin out some stream of consciousness thing, and as long as you appear sincere and sad, they'll take a little pity on you and be less of an asshole. As long as you're not carrying a skateboard or a cardboard sign that reads "god bless" at the end, of course. That's asking for trouble.

She opted for simplicity.

"I saw the light. Door was open."

That part was true.

The old guy stared at her. She almost spoke again, almost opted for the rush-of-confused-words approach, but stopped. She could see this was someone who was going to come to their own decision soon enough.

He smiled at her.

To be accurate, it wasn't a smile. It was more like less of a grimace. But less of a grimace counted as something in Erin's book.

She raised her eyebrows a little, offered a shrug.

"How old are you?" he asked.

She hated that question. Truthfully, no one liked that question, but for her, age was all about when she would be free. Age was one of those things like a secret name that you kept hidden so no one could control you, so no one could judge you, so no one could assume you were a child when you wanted to be an adult, or an adult when you wanted to be a child.

"Truth."

"Eighteen," was her automatic answer, but in a tiny sliver of a second, she knew that he knew it wasn't the truth. Quickly, she added "Next June."

The crazy-haired guy spoke up. "Man, she's just a kid."

Erin ignored him.

The old guy was in charge. She knew it. She kept her eyes on him.

"Shut up," the old guy told the crazy guy, but he never stopped looking at her, either.

He blinked at her for a couple of seconds.

"Seventeen years old and you're out wandering in the woods with those bastards out there? Alone?"

She didn't want to think about "alone" right now. She didn't want to think about why she was alone, why she wasn't arguing over dinner with her sister, why she wasn't mock-moping in the RV, reading and peaceful.

The woman on the couch screamed.

"I'm sorry," said the vet. Tom. She remembered his name.

Erin nodded her chin toward the couch. "Looks like she's awake."

"Goddammit," muttered the old guy.

He turned and stomped into the kitchen.

Nobody moved and nobody said a word, though the woman on the couch moaned a little.

He opened a cabinet high above the refrigerator. Reached in. Pulled out a bottle of Jamieson's.

Stared at it a second.

90

Unscrewed the lid.

"Worst fuckin' night of my life," he muttered and took a long pull.

Introductions Are A Form Of Medicine, Too.

The Jamieson's burned in his throat. It had been six years since he'd had a drink, but this seemed about the right time for it.

As far as drinks go, it wasn't much, maybe a shot and a half. Enough to loosen the strings a bit, but not so much as to mess with his aim...

...and today, aim happened to be a Primary Survival Skill.

He wanted a new day. A day that started yesterday at this same time, that didn't have anything that this day had. A day where, instead of staying home, they decided to go into town for the night. That would have been preferable. That would have been better. That would have been not the Worst Day Ever.

He stared at these strangers in his house, in his home. What a bunch.

There was nothing good here, nothing strong or noble or heroic.

There were haunted looks, blood spatter, people who had lost other people, selfishness, tiredness, weakness, pain, and loss.

He felt all of that, too.

In that moment, Jake realized that if he had left yesterday, gone into town, then none of these people would be here. None of them would have survived this long. Even the tough ones would be dead. He was a pragmatic man in many ways, but he couldn't find it in his heart to be deliberately cruel.

But what about that couple? The ones you were going to push outside?

He shook his head. It was meant to scare them, to get them to shut up. He needed them to stop arguing so he could think. The entire evening had been all reaction and no thinking and that was going to cost.

And hadn't he paid enough tonight?

No, don't think about that.

He sighed.

This was one of those situations where there was a need. They needed him. And as annoying as they were, at least for this night, for this crazy insane bloody night, he needed them, too.

He stepped to the woman on the couch and waved the bottle at her.

"Drink."

She hesitated, so he wiggled it. It was such an absurd gesture, but it worked.

"C'mon, drink some. It won't kill you and I have a feeling you're gonna need it."

She sipped. Coughed.

"Finish it off if you like."

Again, there was a brief hesitation, then she took a longer pull. Still nothing to write home about, but more than the Minimum Required Polite Sip.

He turned to Tom the vet.

"So, what's the verdict?"

"It's broken after all. Not much, but enough to keep her on crutches."

"I don't have crutches. This isn't the kind of a place you can live if you need crutches."

Tom shrugged. "Is this the kind of place where you would have a lot of ibuprofen?"

"Bathroom. Medicine cabinet. Help yourself. Anything else?"

"Just keep her off her feet. She needs a real doctor."

Tom stood up, and cracked his back. "I could use some of that ibuprofen, if you don't mind. I'm too old to be running around being chased by fuckin' monsters. That's a game for teenagers."

Jake watched him head for the medicine.

Then he turned to Jim.

"Okay," he said. "You first." He reached out a hand.

In like Flynn.

Jim took the hand and shook it. "Jim Livingston."

Jim nodded toward the stocky guy. "Brass Gilbert."

Jake nodded toward Brass.

"How's it goin'?" asked Brass.

"Pretty shitty," Jake said without hesitation. "You?"

"'Bout the same. 'Bout the same."

93

Jake turned back to Jim. "And the doc?" he asked.

"Tom Jacoby," said the vet as he walked back into the room. "And I'm not a doc. I'm not even a vet anymore."

Tom crossed the room and knelt at Claire's side.

Jake eyed Jim.

"Why are you out here?" he asked. "No one comes out here."

Jim shrugged and looked around. "Looks like some people do," he said.

"But why?"

"We were, uh, doing a bit of treasure hunting, actually."

Jake shook his head. "Out here? That's crazy. There's nothing out here. Nothing."

Brass spoke up. "It was salvage. Not treasure hunting. Salvage."

"In the old Hatchet Mine," added Jim. "I read somewhere that it never paid out much, but had a lot of interesting antiques strewn around inside."

"Antiques?"

"You know, lights, spikes, tools, whatever. People like antiques."

"And you read this somewhere."

"Yeah. It was a while ago."

Jake ran a hand through his hair. What was left of his hair, anyway. "Son, you go to Hatchet Mine, the only thing you're going to find is your own ass. They dug it a hundred yards in, then a crack loops it right back. Someone sent you on a wild goose chase."

Jim perked up. "You've been there?"

"Sure, and there's no antiques and no treasure. Nothing but rat shit and dust. And every once in a while beer bottles and condoms. Teenagers. I'm assuming those aren't the kind of antiques you're looking for."

"There's nothing? Really?"

"I've been trying to get the County to close it off for almost a decade now. I'm about ready to close it off myself. Tired of cleaning it up after prom night adventures."

"We never found it," said Brass.

"Of course you didn't. You have to go past my house and it's on foot."

"We did find some goddamn big dogs, though," said Jim.

Mark stepped up. "What happened?" he asked.

Jim turned to him. "Nothing special. We got out of the car, unloaded our kits, and followed the trail we thought would go to the mine. Then they came out of the bushes. Lost three people. Started driving. Saw the lights. You know the rest."

Knowing When To Hold 'Em

"What about you, Girl Scout?" Jake asked.

Erin shrugged. "I hate the woods. My family wanted to camp. I was in the camper asleep. They got my family. After they passed by, I got out and followed the light here. That's that."

"That's that?" He could see it in her eyes. Something was missing. *You wanna keep secrets, you keep secrets,* he thought. *Lord knows I have my own.*

"Yeah. And I still hate the woods. Even more now. I mean, c'mon – werewolves? What the fuck, right?"

Mark Gets Lucky

Through the curtained window, Mark saw something. Thought he saw something. A blur or a flash. Something dark on dark.

The front door rattled with an impact and the hardware rang and chattered.

"Jesus, they're at the front door again," shouted Mark.

Jake moved fast toward the door, shoving Mark aside.

"It really is rocket science to you, isn't it," the old man told him.

What the fuck is that supposed to mean?

Something slammed into the door again. This time, the impact shook the wall.

Sean screamed. Not a Serious Problem scream, a What Woke Me Up scream. Mark turned to Deedee and she stared back as she ferociously rocked Sean. *Jesus, that's not rocking him, that's giving him a continuous concussion,* he thought.

He hated when Deedee got stressed out – it was obvious she took it out on Sean. God knows what he's going to be like when he gets old enough to understand what she's saying. On the other hand, I guess that's not a thing I'm going to have to worry about – that's what mental health care professionals are good for.

A third impact against the door.

The red-haired chick – Rose – joined Jake at the front door.

"How strong's that door?" she asked.

"Door's oak. Cabin's oak," said Jake. They both were ready to shoot anything that came through, but even after the third beat, the door was not budging.

Mark saw the movement out front again and this time he was sure. *What the hell are you guys doing out there?* He leaned toward the glass.

He felt Deedee come up behind him.

"What do you see?" she asked. She was asking in *that* voice. The voice he hated hearing because it was a voice that said he was incompetent.

"I don't know, I thought—"

The glass shattered.

Somehow Deedee managed to jump back, out of harm's way, but also somehow, harm's way involved broken glass trying to cut through the curtains and plant seeds in Mark's face.

He screamed something. He wasn't sure what it was, but he knew something angry and surprised came out of his throat.

And then he heard the growling and saw the curtain jerking back and forth.

He jumped back, and the stocky guy, Brass, jumped right in, grabbing the curtains and yanking them down and away.

Bars! Holy shit – the windows were barred. A grid of thin welded bars covered the whole window.

"All right!" he shouted, because triumph in the face of almost being chomped was a glorious triumph indeed.

The picture window was filled with faces. Snarling, teeth-filled animal faces that wanted to bite.

Brass shot from about a foot away.

That was glorious.

Inside, the boom was impressive and inside, he saw the wolf's head split and then burst open. It fell from the window.

Another replaced it.

This one was closer to the front door, snapping a yard away from Mark.

"C'mon, get out of the way!" Rose pushed him aside, aimed, and blew the thing's head inside out.

Damn, that's loud. His ears rang.

"Jake, how strong are the bars?" she called out.

"Stronger than the door."

She shot another one. As it fell away, it was replaced.

98

Jim pushed in toward Jake. "Hey, I can watch the door," he said. "You want to help out there?"

He and Jake traded places. Then Jake grabbed his arm. "Hey."

"What?"

"Don't shoot the door."

"What?!"

"The door. Don't shoot it. I like that door."

"Okay, I won't shoot it."

Another one hit the front door, and the front door held.

Electrons, More Or Less

The baby was screaming.

That's the downside to babies. They scream. They scream and they cry and they make noise. They are vulnerable. They are small and pink and soft. They can't carry a gun and they can't shoot. They need an arm to hold. Everybody can hear them and they drive everybody around them nuts. That's what babies are all about. Screaming and drooling and shitting and driving everybody nuts. Still, I would have. I wanted to. Oh god, I wanted to.

There was a click.

Jake recognized that click. That was an empty gun type of click.

Brass's shotgun was wedged into the mouth of one of those things, and he was squeezing the trigger, but nothing was happening. Specifically, the wolf's head wasn't exploding like it ought to.

Instead, it pushed harder through.

It's bending the bars!

And then it stopped bending the bars, because its head had cracked open. Jake blinked. Brass had pinwheeled the shotgun, and buried the stock in the thing's head.

Wait a sec...

Jake reached into his pocket and fished out a handful of twelve gauge shells. "Hey!"

Brass looked up.

Jake slapped the shells into Brass's hand.

"We don't have to resort to clubs yet."

Snip-snap and the shotgun was reloaded.

Simultaneously he and Brass both swung back to the open bars. This time, two wolves dropped.

"How much more do you have?"

Blam!

"There's plenty more where that came from. Don't be shy."

Boom.

Always when one dropped, another would thrust past the body, crashing into the bars, reaching with tooth and claw.

Two rapid shots, wolf-things squealing.

"Clip!"

Jake turned. That was Rose. Her hand was raised into the air and as he focused on her, a clip landed in the open palm. In a smooth curve, she slammed it into her pistol just as the previous empty hit the floor.

...the hell...?

Jake tracked back across the room.

Carter, her fella, closing that big bag he had slung over his shoulder.

That bag. I wanna know more about that magical bag that produces full clips. I want to see inside that bag and see what other—

"They're coming through!" shouted Brass.

"Shit! Shit! Give me a second." Jake thought hard, looking around.

Brass and Rose were plugging away at them, but there were too many. Even with Jake's shotgun, it was a holding pattern at best. *If they would get away from the bars, we'd have a chance.*

Then he saw the lamp.

"I know what to do, I know what to do!" he shouted, and jumped at the lamp. Damn, this was an ugly lamp, and he always knew it, but sometimes you keep hold of ugly things because your friends give it to you and you think you'll get rid of it as soon as you can, but it kinda grows on you and the next thing you know, your relatives are arguing about it during your wake.

Not this lamp.

He yanked it out of the socket and smashed it against the table.

All lamps look the same when they're naked. All lamps are wires in a tube.

He clamped a foot over the switch mechanism, and pulled upward. The wires snapped free.

"Cover the front!"

He shoved one end of the wire into his mouth and stripped a good four inches of insulation from it. Stripped the other wire the same way. Split the cord.

Tossed it to Brass. "Wire up the bars. Rose, cover him!"

She switched to the area near Brass. Four rapid bursts and the spot was clear.

"Front door's giving out!" Jim warned.

Brass twisted one of the wires around an exposed bar.

Jake turned to Jim. "You shoot it yet?"

"No."

"Good. Then it's not giving out. It's shaking. Watch it!"

Rose fired twice more, clearing a path for Brass.

He twisted the second wire to the other side of the bars.

"You ready yet?"

"Almost, almost..."

Finished the pigtail.

"Done!"

"Okay stand back. Everybody stand back."

Jake had the plug in one hand, holding it right at the wall socket.

"Back away from the bars, goddammit!"

As a unit, Rose, Brass, and the others backed away.

"We're clear," shouted Rose.

The metal grid filled with gray and black faces.

Jake shoved the plug into the socket.

For an instant, he thought that nothing happened. There was no sound, there was no spark.

And then he felt the thing moving through his hands, like a hum that was too deep to hear, but still pinched his fingers as it passed. Even the air felt strange right then, thin and crisp.

Then the sparks came. The howls and the sparks and the flash and the blue afterimage.

And the dark. The silent dark. No one even breathed.

"Holy balls," whispered Rose.

Then the baby screamed.

"Jesus, can't you keep him quiet?" Mark asked.

"I'm surprised *you're* not crying," said Deedee.

Jake closed his eyes. *The broken-leg woman needs the Jamieson's more than I do,* he told himself. *But dammit, it's a close call.*

He opened his eyes. It was still dark, but not *that* dark.

"You need to go into one of the other rooms," he said. "All three of you, because I'm about nine seconds from stuffing a sock in each of your mouths."

The woman looked shocked.

Seriously, no one's offered to do the world that particular favor before? thought Jake.

The three of them vanished into the back.

So Much for Navigation

The cabin sat in the clearing. Near the front window lay a pile of gray bodies. Moonlight made everything silver, including the cabin. Three dead cars clung to each other, oozing vital fluids into the packed-dirt road.

The windows were dark.

In the trees, shapes moved.

Better Late Than Never

In the dark, a match sputtered to life.

Tom held the match up. Looked around.

"On the plus side, looks like they got scared off."

Jake nodded. "For now."

"Yeah, for now. I have a feeling they'll be back."

"We better be ready."

Jim cleared his throat. "Do you have flashlights?"

Something clicked near the ceiling. Dim lights came on.

"I have emergency lights," said Jake.

"I guess that makes this an emergency," muttered Tom.

Reassessing

It watched the cabin from the edge of the trees. It had a vague sense of what the sparking meant. Some distant memory. It meant danger. It meant keep away.

Another one came to it, sat, and waited.

They glanced at each other. The other was jet black, invisible in the night. Not like this one. Not streaked. None of the others were streaked. This was the only one. The hybrid. The First.

So, the others followed Streak, instead of spreading. They all felt the need to spread, but there was something about Streak that compelled them, something that attracted them, something that felt like...

(pack!)

...that felt like being together was better, that being grouped was better.

For now.

Streak turned back to watch the cabin in the dark distance. There was some light now, but not much.

A figure sat in one of the smaller windows, looking out.

Tick-Tock

Erin stared out the window.

She wasn't sure if she could see something out there or not, but she assumed there was something out there and if so, maybe it would be unnerving to stare it down anyway.

Jim stepped over. Not speaking. Also looking out into the dark. That was a relief. Sometimes it's nice when people sit for a minute before talking.

She counted to eighty before he spoke. Not bad.

"You okay?" he asked.

"Yeah."

"It's Erin, right?"

She nodded.

"It's a good name."

They stared out for a while longer.

"What do you see out there?" he asked.

She took a deep breath.

"Planning."

He nodded. "We should be doing that."

"Better hurry."

Tom stepped over. Squinted through the glass. "Dark," he observed. "I thought you might want to know, our fraulein's awake. In a lot of pain, but she can talk."

No Signal

Claire sat up in the couch. One leg curled under, one leg braced horizontal with pillows. She was pale and shook a bit.

Carter and Rose sat at her side.

Jim stepped up, Tom and Jake behind him.

"Do you have a phone?" she asked.

"No phone, sorry. How are you?" he asked.

She turned to Jake.

"Do you have a phone here?"

Jake shook his head. "Never had one installed."

"I have a phone. You wanna use it?" Mark stood on the outside of the ring, near the door leading back into the cabin.

"Yes, please!" said Claire.

He tossed his cell to her.

Eagerness, then confusion, and then a sadness.

The screen read "no signal."

She handed it back.

"The screen's also cracked, too, and a couple of the buttons don't work, and the only game I have on it is—"

"Does anyone have a phone that *works?*" she asked.

Jake shrugged. "I doubt it. No one in the valley, anyway, unless someone has a land line I don't know about. Sorry, but part of wanting to be isolated is being isolated."

"Does anyone know where the nearest phone is?" she asked.

"Over the meadow and through Werewolf Woods," said Mark. "We were planning to take a short drive there just as you arrived. Kinda messed that plan up."

Rose looked up. "Mark..."

Jake growled "You're not helping."

"It's true, isn't it? Now if we want to get out, we have to hoof it and that means either we do a lot of shooting or we throw it some nice distracting meat. Maybe something that can't run so fast. I was thinking we might have to—"

Jake moved in, pressed his face against Mark's. "I think if you want to keep talking, you're going to be talking outside."

Supposed To Be A Security Feature

Carter knelt down next to the woman.

"I'm sorry," he said. "No phone. How are you feeling?"

She rubbed her head.

"I'm tired."

"That might be the ibuprofen. How's your foot. Does it hurt?"

"I feel it, but it doesn't hurt much if I don't move."

"Yeah, that makes sense." He looked into her eyes. "How's your head feel? Are you feeling dizzy?"

"Not dizzy. Tired."

Maybe she had a concussion, maybe not. Carter didn't know. *Probably doesn't matter at this moment,* he thought. *It's not as if we'll rush her to a doctor.*

"What do you remember?" he asked. "Do you remember crashing?"

"I crashed?" she asked. She closed her eyes. "I remember... I remember a car. I tried to go around, but I couldn't. I couldn't steer."

"It's a narrow road."

"No, I mean I couldn't steer. The steering wheel. It was locked."

"Locked? What happened?"

She looked shocked. "The keys. He had the keys in his pocket. He had the keys in his pocket and then they came out of the trees and then he was gone and I didn't have the keys. I coasted."

She looked up.

"I tried to brake, but nothing worked. He had the keys. How could they eat him? They ate both of them. How could they do that?"

Carter shrugged.

"Was that your car?" she asked.

"One of them was."

"Oh, I'm so sorry," she said. After a moment, she added "Can I rest? I don't know if I can go back to sleep, but I think I need to lay back down."

Carter helped her down.

Double-Checking

Rose stood and nodded at Carter. They stepped into a corner.

She touched his arm. "How you doing, baby?" Her voice was low.

Carter nodded. "Good, good. All things considering."

"How are *we* doing?"

"On supplies?"

"On supplies."

"I don't want to take everything out and count, but I would say maybe we have about two-thirds left. Could have more or less, but that's my guess."

"That was my guess, too."

"Looks like our host has his own supply, too."

"Sure, sure, but we gotta pay our own way."

"I agree, but it's one of those things that are good to know. Just in case"

She smiled. It was her Planning Smile. "Just in case."

More Planning

Across the room, Erin crouched in a corner, against the wall.

She was small, not hurt, and a teenager. People ignored her. Most of the time that was what she wanted. Now, it was perfect.

She watched the couple talking in the other corner. The red-haired gal and her guy. They didn't look like trouble, but they looked like something else. Maybe something useful to know.

Erin noticed how every twenty seconds or so, the woman scanned the room. Not casually, though. It looked casual, but it wasn't. It was monitoring.

Erin appreciated that. This was something she did all the time, but she had never seen an adult do it. Maybe adults didn't do it, and that saddened her, because there was a lot to learn shutting up and watching and listening. Apparently, not all adults lost this ability, though.

She watched Rose.

"It's How We Keep Everything
from Happening All At Once."

Time passed and everyone kept to themselves and their own secrets.

But as there is no abandoned factory whose windows don't call out for rocks from passing children, there is no silence human beings encounter such that breaking it doesn't offer some value, however ephemeral.

Frame of Reference

Deedee knelt next to Claire on the couch.

"Hey," she said.

Claire looked up.

"I'm glad you're awake."

"Thank you," said Claire.

"Is there anything you need? Anything I can get you?"

"Mostly, I was hoping to find a phone."

Deedee shrugged. "Wouldn't that be nice?"

"I want to call home. Talk to my mother. Talk to my boyfriend. Hear their voices."

Deedee nodded.

"My mother died," she said.

"Oh no," said Claire. "I'm sorry."

"Don't be – it was a long time ago. I came home from school and she was dead."

"From school? How old were you?"

"Thirteen. Not my best year."

"That must have been terrible."

Deedee shrugged. "I don't know if it was terrible. I mean, she was kind of a bitch. I preferred it when she wasn't home. She would be gone, with one guy or another. I could come home, do my homework, eat something, and go to bed. Usually, that was a good night. When she was home, it was either with a guy and I was a thing she had to excuse and control, or it was without a guy and I was a thing that kept her from being happy. In either case, I tended to take most of it on my back and my head by staying curled up."

Claire was horrified. "You had no father there?"

Deedee laughed. "If I had a father, he was long, long gone," she said. "Sorry, but that's the thing with guys. Under no circumstances should you depend on them for anything at all that matters to you."

"Not all guys are like that. My boyfriend, he's a good person. Always been a good person."

Deedee patted her on the arm. "You're sweet," she said. "But don't get carried away. You think talking to him will help. You think hearing his voice will help. But I don't think you get it. Guys won't help. They *say* they can. They like to *think* they can. But they won't. Believe me, when push comes to shove, guys don't do shit."

As if on cue, Mark walked into the room. He was trying to hold Sean and soothe him, but the baby was in a mood and trying his best to claw Mark in the face. She could tell he loathed Sean. She knew he loathed her and honestly, if there was no Sean, then there would be no them, but instead, she made the best of it. Still, she could hold her loathing until Sean was out of the house. Maybe.

She turned back and Claire was looking at her. Sad.

"What?" she asked.

"Do you think you will always have a chance to make the wrong things right?" Claire asked.

Deedee's head started humming. She knew what that meant. She felt it most of the time when Mark talked to her. She felt it when her old school counselor talked to her. And she felt it when her psych talked to her. It was her body, responding, pushing back against some asshole who was thinking they were so high and mighty and talking down to her. Every time she felt it, she knew someone was trying to make her feel crappy or stupid, and every time she felt it, she knew that they wanted something from her. It wasn't always obvious, but it always turned out to be something.

She stood up.

"Fine, fine. See if I offer *my* help again."

Briefly Unmonitored

In the night, the cabin's windows glowed from battery-powered light.

Figures moved around inside. Some moved in a nervous way. Others moved deliberately.

Outside the cabin, beneath the dark trees, hidden eyes watched them.

Dominance Games

Streak watched Gray, and calculated. Gray was bigger and faster. Gray had already struck. Streak wasn't hurt, but it was the first real challenge to his leadership of the pack...

...there is no more pack – there is only the mission...!

...so it startled him, threw him for a loop.

But he was back. And Gray wasn't going to have a second chance.

Moonlight filled the clearing with icy silver light as the two beasts circled each other. As far as the eye could see, the forest floor was covered with creatures, sitting, and waiting. Dozens, maybe a hundred. All watching.

You should be running, you should be spreading!

They all heard the voice in their head, the voice from inside their new blood, but they ignored it, because there was another voice that felt even stronger, a voice that felt right, and that voice told them...

...there is nothing more important than the pack...

...things that made more sense than the strange commands to run and bite and claw and spread.

So, they waited and watched.

Gray lunged again, and Streak was already gone from the spot.

Maybe not faster...

Streak nipped Gray's ear and Gray yipped.

Gray spun again, snapping with wide jaws, and Streak had already moved behind him.

Another nip.

Streak knew Gray wasn't going to win. He knew that it was important that Gray understand this, though, because if he didn't, then Streak would have to keep tagging him on each lunge and while Gray might not be faster, he was most certainly larger, a bit stupider, and had a lot more stamina. Plus, all things considered, there was no more time for this.

Gray lunged again, but instead of dancing out of the way, Streak leaped straight into the air, spinning, and landed on Gray's broad shaggy back. It was a trick from another life. Before everything changed, this was how Streak fought. Before he was Streak.

Gray stumbled at the weight change.

Streak grabbed fur in clumps and drove his open mouth down against the top of Gray's neck.

Gray spun and twisted, but Streak remained clamped to his back, fingers curled into fur and mouth covering his neck. Three times he rolled and still Streak stayed attached.

Finally, Streak's teeth broke through the skin. Not much, but enough to stop Gray.

Belly down, Gray lay, his head pressed to the pine-needle floor of the clearing, while Streak's teeth hovered above him, at the edge of broken skin.

Grey knew.

He whined.

For a fraction of a second, Streak didn't move. It would never have occurred to either of them that this was a deception, but still, there was a moment of *be sure*.

Then Streak released Gray.

The bigger monster bounded up, turned, and faced Streak. Lowered his head.

Then he ran off into the pack, knowing his place.

Whispers

Everyone else had explored the rest of this cabin, Erin figured it was about time she did, too.

After all, hadn't that been her original intention, to find a solid place to hunker down and wait for this business to pass? So, snooping was utterly justified.

A paneled hallway – *no one misses the Seventies, right,* she thought – led her back and around three corners. Several quiet doors, but one at the end of the hall intrigued her. Light came from it. Also sound. Voices.

She crept closer, listening.

Two men. Low voices.

Glasses. Thick glasses. Booze? *Really? Now?!*

She recognized Jake's voice first. That gravel was unmistakable. The other voice took a second, but then she recognized Jim.

"That's crazy talk," said Jake. "And that's the kind of crazy talk upon which I can speak with authority."

"You can't deny it would explain a lot of things," said Jim. "What they are, where they came from?"

"Look, people buy into that government conspiracy shit because they're saps, and because it's too damn hard to consider the possibility that the world is complicated and sometimes bad things happen. I get that. And believe me when I tell you my entire *generation* gets that. But this is no secret government conspiracy."

"I know what you're saying, but still, I can't get the feeling that this whole thing, that all of us, are going to end up somewhere in a numbered file in an office that claims to be the FBI."

"Oh, hell yeah. Don't get me wrong, son. I don't think they *caused* it, but that don't mean they won't find a way to take *advantage* of it. That don't mean some lackey with a shock stick isn't going to be hired to drop these things into unfriendly territory by some spook. There is no government on the planet that isn't competing to be the biggest asshole on Earth."

"If they catch us...?"

"Yeah, don't think that thought hasn't crossed my mind, too. I think we've been lucky as shit so far."

Someone tapped Erin's shoulder and she jumped. Turned.

Deedee grinned a skeleton grin. "Hey," she whispered. "You snoopin'? Not nice."

She pushed past Erin and into the room.

Man Cave

One whole wall was lined with books.

Deedee had never seen so many books before. In her whole life she had read maybe six books.

The bed looked normal, and the rest of the room looked normal, but Jesus, it was like some kind of room devoted entirely to books.

Jim stood at the bookshelf, his back to her, staring at the books.

Jake sat near a small table at the foot of the bed. He leaned back, his hands behind his head. He looked lost at first, but scowled as she entered.

"What do you think our chances are?" asked Jim, without turning around.

"Hi!" she said. "Whatcha talking about?"

Jim turned and started to speak. "We were talking about—" but he stopped at a look from Jake.

Deedee waited a second. "What?" she asked. "Go on, what were you talking about?"

Jim didn't answer.

Jake stared at her. She didn't like that stare. Not one bit.

"Well, what were you talking about?"

Still the silent treatment.

She knew how to handle this kind of horseshit.

She turned to Jake and put her hands on her hips.

"This is your place, so you're in charge."

Jake stared. Didn't nod or anything.

"What are you doing to help?" she asked. "I mean it, what are you doing? Because I see a whole lot of not doing anything and a whole lot of bad things outside, so I want to know what you're doing to protect us in *your* house."

Most of the time, once you lay things out like that, people start talking. If they don't, then she kept going until they did.

But something in Jake's eyes was colder. When he blinked, it didn't seem like he was blinking, but that he was taking a brief moment to decide whether or not to kill you.

Deedee stepped back. Somehow she couldn't help herself on that.

"What?" she asked.

No, no, I sound so weak, so wavery. I sound like someone who's cowed by this silent treatment shit. I am not. I can't let him push me around. I got rights! I ought to—

"You see," said Jake. "We were talking." His voice was level. Scary-level.

"Yeah, about what?"

But she knew. *I lost it. I can't believe I lost it right here with that old guy. He didn't move a goddamn muscle and he pushed me right away.*

She was sick with shame and fury, but shame was winning.

"We. Were. Talking," repeated Jake.

She felt the push as if it was physical. Took another step back.

"Fine," she said.

I am not fine. Nothing here is fine. No one here is fine.

"Fine. First that crazy foreign woman and then that little creeper wandering around the house all silent, and now you two. No one has a fucking clue what we're going to do, do they?"

The men exchanged a glance.

That fucking glance. She hated that glance with a passion that burned iron. That glance that men offered each other when they felt pity, when they thought "There's a nice gal who's lost her shit. Too bad – she still had a few good years left in her."

This, she told herself, *has been totally unproductive.*

She turned and left them to their boy games, to their clubhouse, to their fancy books.

123

In The Heart

The room was dark, but Erin knew it was important, she could feel it was important. It exuded a sense of vitality.

She felt for a light switch and flipped it on.

Oh, it was important.

One whole wall was the generator.

An old computer, an old printer, a typewriter, reams of paper, file cabinets, reference books, maps, diagrams, a dry-erase board filled with tiny often-erased-and-redrawn lines and arrows, newspaper clippings, and more. Old cups holding skins of dried coffee, plates forgotten behind stacks of documents, pencils chewed until they were mangled sticks.

That was one wall.

The other wall was the product. The lovely product.

Practical Approaches to Anarchy.

The Predatory State.

Dismantling Hierarchies.

Each book was hand bound in one of those old-fashioned spring-powered binders. The title was hand-printed on the spine in perfect block letters.

Erin's eyes spotted right away a spine-cracked copy of *The Laws of the Jungle*. That should have been obvious.

There were more. Books from the dark side of publishing. Books written by people who used their initials. Books with tiny print runs. Books that contained dangerous, dangerous things.

Some of the titles she recognized. Some she had read, some she had only heard of. And some she had never heard of, but which tantalized her through their titles alone.

There were textbooks.

From high-school level books through college and more. Mathematics, Physics, Chemistry, Astronomy, Law, Medicine, Mechanics, Economics, everything. She shook her head. To read all of these books would take a lifetime.

Then she looked back at the hand-written spines.

She turned back to the generator side of the room.

Saw the binders there, the empty binders waiting for their books to be written.

In the typewriter, a half-written page beckoned, so she looked.

> *The fundamental breakdown occurs in the act of separation, the exquisite dehumanizing moment of separation, when we are told to see others as Others. When we are told that they are alien, strange, vile, and despicable. They are not, and it is an act of deep humility and grace to see those Others as ourselves, in other skins and other minds. The essential nature of the Universe is gravity, every object pulling on each other with a force proportionate to its mass, and this is no different with emotions, with the psyche, with the feelings that we normally think of as friendship and love. No different at all.*

It was page eighty-three.

She looked at the wall near the desk, at the pictures there.

A framed copy of the Declaration of Independence.

No surprise there, she thought.

The rest of the pictures were people. Jake as a boy, eyes filled with defiance. Jake as a young man, eyes filled with determination. Jake with a college degree held high in one arm, while the other arm was wrapped around another graduate, a woman with an arresting stare. More pictures of Jake and the woman. Sometimes in strange places, sometimes with signs and placards, sometimes facing armored police, on marches, and, as they grew older, sometimes alone together. In all the pictures, the two people shared the same steel in their eyes, the same fire.

She leaned closer to look at the latter ones. Still the same couple. Still alone.

She heard something behind her. Something quiet.

She blinked, working though possible responses. Only one stood out as either a winner or a loser. The rest were losers.

In a steady, even voice, she said "No time for kids."

She turned her head.

Jake stood there.

He was much closer than her comfort zone, but she wasn't going to push, because she was completely aware of the fact that she was inside *his* comfort zone. So far inside his comfort zone that there aren't a lot of scales of "trouble" that go this high.

She could see surprise. Not much, but for a second, he was surprised she knew he was there.

And then he heard what she said. Really heard it.

His face fell.

Oh god, she thought. *No, no, I didn't want to hurt him. Oh, no! I just wanted to throw his balance off. I had no idea...*

He took a deep breath and his mask was back on. Stoic.

"No time," he said.

It was a punt and she knew it. She had bought passage this far.

"So, what happened?"

That wasn't going to work and she knew it as soon as she said it.

"What are you looking for?" Jake asked.

Damn, he has that look again, she thought.

She nodded toward the bookcases, the bookshelves, the workspace.

"Every house has a place where the precious things are kept."

"This room'll do."

"Fireproof?"

"Once the door is closed, maybe, but I wouldn't trust it, myself. The front door is stronger. Whatever gets through the front door will get through here eventually."

She nodded. "If they know something's in here," she said. "One person can be very, very quiet. Sometimes the best security is to hide in plain sight, but not be as visible."

Jake raised an eyebrow at her. "You're talking about hiding," he said. "Good. You want to be talking about hiding, because you absolutely do *not* want to be talking about anything more troubling than that. Hiding I understand. You seem good at it. But don't be evil."

"Hiding." It was true. As soon as he spoke, she knew what he meant, and that was not what she had been planning at all. That would be evil, indeed.

"Good. We're clear."

"We should be. So..." she straightened up, facing the bookshelves. "What made you write all this?"

Jake stepped aside and gestured at her to leave the room.

Time to play through, she thought, and stepped out.

After she stepped out, he followed. He locked the door behind him and dropped the key in his breast pocket.

"Someone had to," he said.

Pawns

In the dark, Streak watched the cabin.

Gray shapes slid along the ground, hunching lines of attack, closing in on the wooden walls.

Streak growled.

No more waiting.

The Word

Jim sat at the window, looking out, lighting his cigarette.

I guess if there were two more people, I could worry about lighting three to a match, but it's not as if we have snipers out there, so that's a useless piece of trivia I'll never need from my high school history class.

He glanced at Rose and Carter, sitting in one corner, talking with each other.

Home would be nice. I wouldn't mind being home at all, he thought. *I could call Kim. Yeah, I don't know her well, but at least it would be a voice glad to hear from me.*

Someone he could say hi to, and not be asked about when he was going to sell the house and how they were going to split the costs and the profits. His ex was civil, but hers was not a voice he wanted to talk with.

"Hey."

Tom had crept up from behind, startling him.

"Jesus, Tom!"

"Sorry. I figured you knew I was coming what with your eyes being open and you looking around and stuff."

"Looks can be deceiving."

"Apparently. Give me a cigarette."

Jim handed him the pack. Only three left anyway. Tom pulled one out with his thin fingers and handed the pack back.

He nodded at the collection of fresh butts on the windowsill.

"Nice job."

"Thanks. I thought you quit."

Tom lit up, and pulled deep. That did the trick.

"I made a decision to stop worrying about the long-term effects on my health," he said. "Just being practical. Is that your last pack?"

"Last pack. There's more in the car."

Tom nodded. "You got two left."

129

Tom glanced at Claire. Jim followed his gaze. She stared out a window.

They both looked at Mark and Deedee sitting at the dinette. Their body language said they were trying to figure out how to eat the baby and blame each other for it. Deedee caught Tom looking and stared back at him, grimacing.

Tom looked back at Jim. Shook his head.

"It's gonna be one long-ass night," he said.

Jim nodded. "Already is."

Carter stepped over. Nodded at the two of them.

"Gentlemen," he said.

Jim wanted to like Carter, but something about the man made him uneasy. Normally, that could be ignored. Normally.

He offered the cigarette pack to Carter.

"No, no thanks," said Carter.

He leaned down and looked out the window into the dark.

"What's the word?" he asked.

"Fucked," said Tom. "The word is most definitely 'fucked'."

Over His Head

Carter stared at Tom until Tom blinked.

"Thanks for the smoke, Jim," he said, and stepped away.

Carter watched him as he walked away.

"Interesting guy," he said.

"Tom speaks his mind. I appreciate that about him. I guess sometimes he's a bit... clumsy, but I never get the sense he's hiding anything," Jim said.

Carter shrugged. Looked back out the window.

"Been quiet out there, huh?"

Jim thought *You're probably a nice guy, but damn, you couldn't take a hint if it was handed to you in a cake box.*

"Thought I saw something on the edge of the road a couple hours ago," said Jim. "But who's to say. Maybe it was something, maybe it wasn't. Maybe the electricity fried their brains. Maybe they won't be back."

"That would be great, wouldn't it? So, nothing so far?"

"Haven't heard anything. Haven't seen anything."

Carter nodded. "You think we ought to make a run for it?"

Jim stared at the man. "Are you insane?"

"No, I'm serious. I think we might have enough ammunition. I'm not so sure we have enough house."

Jim shrugged. "Seems sturdy to me."

"Sturdy? You saw what they've done to the front door. You think that's gonna last?"

Jim didn't say anything. He didn't have to.

"Exactly. We need to figure out a plan of some kind, and roll it out. Because sitting in a cabin and waiting for the walls to fall is a shitty plan. At least by my lights."

Jim looked back out into the dark. Shook his head.

"I don't know," he whispered. "Honestly, I don't know."

131

"What do you mean you don't know? Aren't you one of the guys who's in charge of this circus?"

Jim ran a hand though his hair. No wonder it was thinning. "No, no, I can't be in charge. Not of this. This is too big."

"What do you mean, man. You were in charge of a whole gang, and you did a pretty good job of that, from what I can see."

"Carter, I set up the trip. If it was softball, or miniature golf, or a hike, I'm okay making those kinds of decisions, but not this. This is life-or-death. This is crazy."

"But someone's gotta do it. We need people to look up to. That's a fact of life."

"No, I can't. I can watch. I can report. But I can't be in charge. It's bad enough I have to talk to three widows when I get back."

"Two widows."

They both turned at the new voice. Brass sat nearby. Listening. Cleaning a gun. "Sidney wasn't married. Two widows."

Jim closed his eyes and nodded. "Right. Thanks."

Orders

In the dark, the shapes moved.

Stripe growled and snuffled and used the blood talk.

They didn't want to go near the cabin again. The blue light had hurt their eyes and the touching caused pain. They learned that lesson.

Stripe pushed hard.

They whined, but they slunk away. He knew they would do it. He knew this would work.

In The Wrong Hands

Jake's shotgun lay against the wall near the front door. It was an old model, with a stock worn until it was shiny, but it shot straight. Jake owned this shotgun since he was twenty-seven.

Ten seconds later, it was no longer there.

Remembering The Bei Chez Heinz

Jake found Claire staring out the window. He sat next to her and stared, but it was as dark out this window as it had been out other windows.

He gave her a minute to become accustomed to his presence.

"Where you from?"

She sighed. "Germany."

"No, no, I mean, what city?"

She turned to him, raising an eyebrow. He continued. "I ask because of the way you say your R's. *Hoch Deutsche*, right?"

She smiled a little. "Hanover," she said. "I'm from Hanover."

He nodded. "Only place I been where they still speak it. Everywhere else, they sound popular."

"You've been there?"

"Long time ago. Long, long time ago. I never could get the R right."

"Did you like it there?" she asked.

"I used to hang out a lot at a place. Hm..." he closed his eyes and thought. "It was called the Bei Chez Heinz. Kind of a hippy sort of place. I guess it's been there since forever. I heard they stopped playing music and went under."

Claire's eyes lit up. "No, no," she said. "I showed photographs there. They still play music, too, but they also show art."

"Well, they used to have art there, and sometimes people would play music. Then it became all music all the time, I guess. So, now they're back to art?"

"And music. Many concerts there. It's very crowded often."

"It was intense back then, too."

Claire nodded. "It's a good place. Good people run it."

"Still the DGB, or someone else?"

"No, not the DGB anymore. Someone else. And it moved. That part of town wasn't helping things."

"That explains why it's so much more popular now, huh?"

"It is."

"And it's still a good place, right? Still worth a night out?"

"Oh, always, yes. Still good."

They both stared out the window, but Jake saw her eyes remembering happy things for a moment, and that was a good thing.

"Sorry I have no phone," he said softly.

She shrugged. "Can't be helped."

Trail of Destruction

The cabin was deeper than it looked.

"About time you showed up," hissed Deedee. "You find it?"

Mark waved the shotgun at her. "By the front door, like you said."

"Be quiet – they're going to hear us."

"They're not going to hear us – they're all the way at the other end of the house. Besides, I *am* quiet. Now if *you* can shut up for once in your life, we might be able to pull this off."

She stared at Mark.

"Fuck you."

"Yeah, yeah, promises, promises. How about we wait until after we escape before we start talking about rewards?"

On one hand, he hated that look.

On the other hand, he loved that he could still get her goat.

More Echoes

Erin couldn't figure Brass out. He *seemed* sturdy, self-contained.

She sat next to him.

He nodded to her.

"You're pretty much on top of things with your boss over there," she said, indicating Jim.

Across the room, Jim stared out of the window. Worried. He smoked his last cigarette.

Brass took a deep breath. "Erin, is it?"

"Yeah."

"Everybody needs somebody, Erin."

She felt a flare inside, a burst of emotions. Fear, anger, loss. Her sister's exact words.

She kept herself steady.

Dang, looks like it's button-pushing day for everyone, she thought.

"Sometimes we get lucky," he continued. "Sometimes we learn early on that we don't always do as well alone as we would like to think. Sometimes we learn that what we need to feel right with the world is to be helping others. We might not always have a chance to pick the others we would prefer, but we're rarely in a position to make that choice. Know what I mean?"

Before she could answer, a booming shot rang out.

Pure Evil, Man. Pure Fuckin' Evil.

"What the *fuck?!*" shouted Jake.

In three steps, he was at the front door.

"Where's my shotgun?!"

The baby screamed from the back of the cabin.

Shouts. Protestations. Angrier shouts.

Mark stumbled backwards into the main room of the cabin, in some semblance of a fighting stance, but it was obvious this was a man who couldn't fight his way out of a wet paper bag.

There was a blur and Tom was in the room, full stride.

With a crack, he clipped Mark across the head.

Mark spun, falling to his hands and knees. He made a kind of cry-sob when he hit, not unlike the baby's own cries.

Jim and Jake latched onto Tom, whose face was pure fury.

"Let me go!" roared Tom. "That bastard's going flat, I swear to fucking god, I'm going to hit him until—"

"*Tom!*" shouted Jim.

Tom's head snapped around as if he was smacked, and he stared at Jim. For a fraction of a second, it looked like it was going to be a rare episode of Tom Jacoby Beats Up The Whole Wide World, but then he recognized the people around him.

"You fucker," gasped Mark. "You crazy fucker."

Tom tensed at that, but his arms were now held.

He looked at Jim and at Jake. Then he looked down at Mark. Physically and in every other way possible.

"He was leaving."

"What?!" asked Jake.

"They were going out the back, out the back door. All three of them."

Deedee ran in, Sean wailing in her arms. "He's lying," she said, her words tumbling over each other. "We went to the back to talk. Just to talk. We weren't doing anything wrong. And then all of a sudden this asshole comes back and starts shouting and pushing and hitting."

"I *heard* you. I *saw* you," said Tom.

"We were just *talking*, goddammit," said Mark. His nose bled and the side of his face looked more like a beet than before.

"You were leaving. You had the door open. You were going to walk away and then leave the door open and let those things in, and in the confusion you were going to sneak away."

"That's bullshit," Mark protested.

"You were going to try to make it to your brother's car, and then once you made it there, you thought you would be safe."

Mark shook his head.

"*I heard you!*"

Mark stood up, staggered to Tom.

"Whatever you thought you heard, you're wrong."

He leaned in close. "You fucking nutjob."

Jim thought he had a grip on Tom's arm, but he didn't realize he no longer held that arm until after Mark was already reeling back from the punch.

The shouting rose in a cacophony. Everybody had an opinion, and volume made it more important. Jim managed to grab Tom's shoulder, and then work his way down to the arm, still flailing, still reaching out for Mark's head.

Priority Observations

Erin stayed out of it. She knew better. When people started throwing punches, it was time to leave the area. Time to get out of the way. Nothing good happened after that.

Then she saw Claire.

Claire wasn't watching the fight.

Claire was staring outside.

Staring not at the endless dark that everyone else had been staring at, or at the endless dark that even she had been staring at earlier, but staring at something real.

Something that locked her up in fear.

The Facts Of The Matter

"Everybody. Stop talking *NOW!*" Somehow, Jake's voice managed to cut through everybody else's voice, and silence fell.

Except for Sean, whose cries at least hitched to a stop. Even the baby knew it was Quiet Time.

Deedee smoothed the thin wisps of hair on Sean's head, petting him into peacefulness, insofar as a baby could be peaceful in the middle of an argument. She glared at Tom.

Tom and Mark glared at each other.

Jake put his face into Tom's face.

"You. Keep your shit together."

He pointed at Mark. "You stop talking. Stop talking entirely. I need to sort this shit out now. And that's what you want too, because as of this moment unsorted shit goes outside."

He stepped to Deedee. She backed away, but he stepped right into her space again. This time, she didn't back down.

"Just talking?"

She nodded. "Just—"

"Don't be fancy. Just talking, right? Yes or no?"

"Yes."

Jake nodded.

"Not trying to run out on us at all? Not running out the back door? Not leaving it open?"

"...no..."

Jake moved closer. His face was inches from her. He could smell her, smell her confusion and smell her anger and most importantly, smell her lies. But that wasn't enough. It wasn't enough that he saw it.

I am your fucking storm... he thought.

"Not trying to fuck us...?"

She shook her head, but she was terrified. It wasn't a smooth shake. It was convulsive and fear-filled.

...and I will break upon your dumb-ass shore.

"Then why," he asked quietly, "Did you take my gun?"

He watched it happen. He'd seen it happen before with people like her. People who had no bones in their body, but who whipped others for what bones they had. He'd known her type the instant he'd seen them on the porch and if it hadn't been for the baby, he would never have opened the door. He watched her engines of desperation kick in as she searched for a way out of her own trap.

Her eyes danced back and forth, reflecting her brain's search.

Jake never moved. Never blinked.

She looked at Mark. At anyone other than Jake, but Jake did not stop staring at her eyes.

Finally, with nothing left to do, she looked back into his eyes, and it was all laid out open and plain as day.

"...fuck," she said, in a dry husked voice.

"*Godammit,* Deedee!" said Mark. "Don't talk! Stop talking!"

She turned to him, her face twisting into rage. "It was *your* fucking idea. Your stupid fucking idea!"

This, Jake thought. *This is what they are when they aren't pretending to be human beings.*

She turned to Jake.

"It was his fucking idea," she insisted.

As if that mattered any more.

The Back Door

There's a back door? thought Carter. *This might be a good thing!*

He glanced toward Rose, caught her eye. Motioned with his eyes toward the back door. She nodded.

Most of her attention was on the German girl, however.

Carter slipped into the darkness.

The voices started rising again.

All Signs Point To Bad

Erin watched Claire, but she felt herself tensing. Claire was across the room, and there was no way to call out to shout, or to even ask. This drama in the middle of the room was secondary to whatever Claire was watching, but too noisy to transmit information through.

The only thing she could go on was Claire's physical responses.

Claire's hands shook and her eyes started blinking.

So not good, thought Erin.

"Hey," shouted Rose. "Hey, everybody!"

Most of the shouting died down and everybody looked at Rose...

...who was now looking at Claire.

Terrified Claire.

Claire turned and looked back at everybody.

"Something's happening," she whispered. "They're back."

Every Dance Has A Why

They watched in the dark as the wolves danced.

Into the trees. Out of the trees.

Growling, snapping, yipping, jumping.

None sat still.

Rose shook her head. "What the hell are they doing?"

Every once in a while, one of them would stop and look into the cabin. Not in the direction of the cabin, but *into* the cabin. Rose was sure of it. The wolves were seeing *them*.

"Wish I could say," said Jake.

More than seeing them, Rose thought. *They're looking for something from us. They want our attention. What are they...?*

"I suppose if they're in the open, might as well try to better the odds," said Tom, raising his pistol.

Rose realized what they were doing. It burst in her head like a silent balloon that carried something very dangerous instead of helium. It opened doors of thought in a fraction of a second that filled her with a strange taste. It wasn't rage or anger or determination.

It was fear.

In the instant she figured out what the wolves were doing, she knew they were all going to die.

That was when the glass broke.

Strange Bedfellows

"They're at the back door. Son of a *bitch!*" shouted Jake.

"They distracted us," said Rose. No one heard her except for Erin.

From the back, a half second after the glass broke, a shotgun's boom thundered.

Rose's head jerked as if she'd been shot. "*Carter!*"

A second boom shook the walls.

Carter burst into the room, carrying Jake's shotgun. "Here!" he called to Jake, tossing the gun.

Jake caught it and cracked it open. Two smoking shells flew out.

"It's empty. I had two. They're coming in the back!"

The instant Carter had burst into the room, Rose knew what he needed. Before he finished explaining to Jake, she had Carter's pistol already extended toward him.

"Here, baby," she said. "Shoot the shit out of 'em."

Carter winked at her and took it. Pointed at Jim and Brass. "C'mon. The rest should stay up front and watch the shop, but I need you guys back here now!"

"Hey," said Mark. "Don't leave me here with him." He pointed at Tom.

Jake shoved two fresh shells into the shotgun. Handed it to Mark. "You go where you'll be useful. You thought you could handle this – now's your chance." He fished out a handful of shells from a pocket and gave them to Mark.

More glass broke in the back.

Carter ran for the hall. "*Let's move it!*"

Jim and Brass followed.

Mark hesitated.

"Move it!" barked Jake.

Mark moved it.

147

Built Wolf-Tough

Carter hit the door first, skidding to a stop to assess the situation. It would not do to run right into something trying to eat him.

The door had glass panes, all of which were shattered. Shards of glass littered the floor. Faces and teeth and claws struggled to get past the heavy bars, but failed.

The cabin was intact and the door still closed, despite the wall of fury beyond it.

Carter made sure his patch of floor was clear, and dropped to one knee, drawing a bead on one of the heads at the door.

"I *really* like this house," he muttered.

He squeezed off a shot and with a scream, half a wolf head fell from the window.

Behind his head, he heard a boom and watched as another wolf face vanished in a spiral of viscera.

For a second, he looked back. Both Jim and Brass stood behind him, weapons out, taking aim.

Jim fired and something else at the door screamed.

Carter turned back to the work of picking off monsters.

He Who Hesitates Is...

Mark arrived and the other three men were already firing.

He brought the old shotgun up to bear, but there was no clear shot around Jim or Brass, both of whom were standing.

Mark held the shotgun at ready.

What can I do? I can't shoot through them. I can't shoot around. I can't go back. I can't do anything.

He stepped back. Once. Twice.

A corner. Good. I can stand here. If something happens, then I can come in, I can start shooting, but for now, I can wait and watch and keep an eye on things from back here, back where it's safe.

He took another step backward.

Carpet Bombing

In the dark of the woods, the flashes of light coming from inside the back door provided the sole illumination. But that was plenty. They knew what needed to happen. They must flood into that door, roll through the cabin, and spread into everyone there.

A hundred gray bodies threw themselves at the door.

The shots continued.

Peasant Under Glass

The window was small, but not too small. And inside it was a man, his back to the glass. Gray knew this was something that could be done to restore his position, so he cut away from the main attack and looped wide to get a good run.

Six steps later, he was in the air, heading toward a tiny square of glass, beautifully unbarred.

Flanked

The three men were firing in a hypnotic rhythm, shooting down wolf after wolf.

Mark watched them, unable to grasp this kind of energy and precision.

The gunfire and the snarling and the barking was a continuous act of noise.

It was so noisy that he didn't even notice the extra glass breaking behind him.

But he *did* notice the claw tear across his shoulder. He screamed like a girl.

He spun, bringing the shotgun to bear.

Squeezed the trigger.

Nothing happened.

He shook the gun, while the wolf- thing reached for him again.

The goddamn safety!

He clicked it off, raised the shotgun.

The second clawing missed him, but batted the shotgun out of his hands.

He tripped backward, landing on his ass.

The wolf pulled its head through and started twisting, corkscrewing itself through the window.

A second front paw was through.

A double-shot and wolf's head burst apart.

Mark ducked at the noise, but turned.

Carter and Jim were still firing at the door, methodically blowing monsters away, but Brass was aiming right for the little window. The barrel of his pistol smoked.

Brass returned his attention to the back door.

Mark scrambled to his feet, almost tripped over the gun again, then picked it up.

Pointed it at the window. The muzzle jumped and shook with his arms.

Something furry flashed across his view and without thinking, he fired. *Maybe I got it,* he thought, but then he saw a new chip out of the stone wall two feet from the window.

Still On Plan A

Rose, Jake, and Tom watched the wolves out front, prancing and jumping.

The rattle of gunfire from the back room was dismaying.

"Are they doing *anything?*" asked Rose.

"Just the same game," said Jake.

A Very Special Bullety Event

The back door frame shook. Plaster chipped away here and there.

"Back, back!" called Carter. The men stepped back, still firing.

Beasts kept dropping.

"We're losing it," said Jim. "Seriously, we got maybe a minute."

"Fuck it," said Carter. "*Blitz 'em!*"

They blitzed 'em.

There is a popular phrase used to mean something so overwhelming that there is no chance to respond intelligently. The only option is to respond instinctually, to debase oneself to the level of an animal and respond in that way.

That phrase is "shock and awe."

It's not a useful tactic for most animals, because animals don't have morale. Animals attack for simple and clean reasons. Animals attack when they are defending their young. Animals attack when they are threatened. These are things that don't require morale. They require teeth and claws and stamina. You can't "shock and awe" an animal into no longer defending its young or itself.

In this case, though, these weren't strictly animals. They were something else.

So when the lights flashed from inside the house, and a wide wave of pack fell dead or dying, and that wave of death spread like a wind, Streak felt something he had never felt before.

He was shocked.

He was in awe.

So he howled.

He howled and the others stopped the attack, stopped the rush, even stopped the dancing outside.

155

When Streak howled his frustration and confusion, every beast surrounding the cabin jumped away, drifted into the trees and bushes like gray smoke into darkness.

They vanished.

Super Effective

Carter raised a hand and the other two men stopped firing.

Other than echoes and the ringing of ears, there was silence. No wolves. No nothing.

"It worked," he said. "It fuckin' worked."

"Was a good idea," said Brass. "I wouldn't have thought of it."

"Shit, shit, shit!" said Mark.

They turned to look at him.

He stood behind them in the hallway. His shirt was torn from the first strike, and he held his left arm in his right hand, rubbing it.

A shallow scratch on his arm pulsed and puckered the skin around it.

"One fuckin' scratch, man. Jesus! What the fuck?!"

Clever Girl

Jake stared into the dark. "What the hell was *that* all about?" he asked.

"It was a diversion," said Rose. "It was a diversion and now it's over." She turned to the others. "They know about diversions. Holy shit."

Sometimes People Just Change

Brass burst into the room. "Clear a spot!" he shouted.

Jim and Carter staggered in, Mark hanging between them. Mark moaned and rolled his head around. "Oh shit, oh shit, oh shit," he kept repeating.

Jim shouted "Tom!"

Deedee stood up, staring. Her mouth worked, but no words came out.

"What happened?" asked Tom.

Carter replied "He was scratched. A couple of times."

"Scratched?!"

Mark held out his arm. It was swollen and purple, oozing thin lines of clear pus.

"Jesus," said Tom. "When did this happen? Just now?"

"It looks bad," said Jim.

"No shit it looks bad. It looks unreal. I mean, there's no way this happened a minute ago. This is what I would expect from a week of infection. Maybe more."

Mark grabbed Tom's arm. "It came through the window," he said. "It scratched me, but I'll be fine, right? This shouldn't be a problem, right? Some ibuprofen for the swelling, maybe, or some— *ouch!*"

Mark twitched as Tom pulled Mark's sleeve up.

Black streaks glided under the skin, away from the wound. They flowed up Mark's arm, meeting more coming down.

His skin darkened and somewhere inside his body, something started crackling.

"What?" asked Mark. "It's only a scratch, isn't it? What's that— ah! *Shit!*"

The crackling was soft and liquidy, but grew louder.

Mark's hands shook.

Tom looked at Jim. Jim looked at Jake.

Jake looked grim. "Doesn't take long," he said.

159

"What doesn't take long?" Mark asked. "C'mon, guys, what?"

"Mark...?" said Deedee.

Jim looked at Jake, then Tom. "I don't want to do it," he said. "I can't. I can't."

"Do what?" asked Mark.

"Yeah, do what?" asked Deedee. She touched Mark's cheek.

He looked into her eyes and dark streaks crawled up his chin, crossing his cheeks.

Tom nodded. "Someone has to," he said.

Mark looked into Sean's eyes and Sean gazed back at his father. The baby's eyes were normal – clean, clear, and pure. Mark's eyes streaked with color.

Mark trembled. Fell to his knees. Looked up at Deedee.

"No," she whispered. "No!"

She faced the men. "No, no, you can't do it. Can't you see he's scared?"

Jake said "If we don't—"

"You, especially, shut up. Jesus fucking Christ, ever since we got here, you've been lording everything over our heads like we're some kind of retard, and not once have you treated us decently. Not once have you not pointed a gun at us or threatened us."

Deedee saw that they were moving away from her. Good. When she was intimidating, she was effective.

"You think we *picked* this shithole? You think we *chose* to come and hide here? No, we found it by accident. All of us found it by accident. So that means we all have to work together. We all have to find a way to make it work. So if you could pull your head out of your ass long enough to—"

From behind her, two great clawed hands clamped themselves to either side of her head.

Silence Is Golden

It stood seven feet tall, head scraping the ceiling with wispy gray ear tufts.

For a second, Deedee was confused and voiceless.

Then she started a scream, but it was cut off. More specifically, it was pinched off as her neck twisted around a hundred and eighty degrees. The beast that used to be Mark spun her head to face him.

Her body did not follow, and her snapping neck cracked like a belt.

The wolf held her upright, but her hands and arms twitched. Sean fell to the floor like a wet bag.

On his first bounce, he landed in Claire's hands. Somehow she had seen it coming and lunged from across the room.

The wolf's mouth split wide open, its teeth still extruding, still sharpening.

It bit Deedee's face.

Bone crushed like a cheap ceramic bowl.

In Claire's arms, Sean screamed as his mother's blood pattered down on him.

Dropping the corpse, the beast looked down at the screaming baby.

Claire, gasping in pain, rolled away, shielding Sean with her body.

A massive clawed foot slammed into the floor where Claire's head had been seconds earlier.

She struck a table, bounced off, tried to roll back the other way, and then she stopped as he caught her.

The second foot pistoned down, directly into Claire's abdomen. It thudded against the wooden floor, pulverizing soft tissue and crushing spine en route.

She screamed, but it was as much a convulsion as it was a scream. Blood and other fluids spurted out of her mouth and nose.

Sean slipped from her grasp and rolled to the floor.

The thing fell to all fours. One massive paw swept Sean away like a puck, and the mouth opened across Claire's throat, tearing and ripping.

Three guns fired at the exact same instant – Tom's, Jakes, and Brass's.

The thing that used to be Mark blew apart into several wet red pieces, and fell to the floor.

Going Home

Claire's eyes wandered, staring at the ceiling, as her brain tried to make sense of what happened.

Jake knelt down next to her. Hands on either side of her face. Cradling her. Looking at her.

Behind him, Sean whimpered, and Rose reached down, scooping him up. "C'mon, little man, let's step over here. Let's go look at some stuff over here." She hummed a little song and the baby grew quiet.

Claire's eyes locked on Jake's.

She saw him.

Jake stroked the blood-matted hair from her forehead.

In silence, Claire closed her eyes, and then died.

Jake held her for a moment. He could already see that whatever Claire had been had gone, but still he held her with grace and kindness.

He closed his eyes, bowed his head, and the room was quiet with him.

The Problem

"We can't stay here," said Jim.

Jake's head remained down. "There's nowhere else to go."

"I don't care."

"You're gonna care when they rip your fucking guts out," said Jake. He looked up. "Where you going to go, Jim. You gonna climb a tree? You gonna sprout wings and fly away?"

Carter cleared his throat. "Look, I love this place. You built it tough as shit, and if this were ordinary weirdness, I would be all over sticking around, barricading the door, and collecting corpses as lawn ornaments. But look *around* you, man. They are getting more 'in' every time they hit us. If we stay here, they *will* get in and then we are fucked."

Jake turned on him. "Right, like *you* have all the answers."

"I'm not saying I have all the answers, just that I can *see* what's happening—"

"—what's going to happen next when they—"

"—there won't *be* a next time if we just—"

"—only so many bullets—"

"—it's only glass – they can't cut through walls—"

"—a matter of time—"

"—goddammit, *listen,* you're not thinking straight—"

Rose spoke up. "Hey. *Hey!*"

They all stopped and stared.

She rocked Sean as she spoke. Her voice remained gentle and soothing to the listening baby, but her words came out like ice. "Stop dicking off. This is not solving anything. We need to *solve* something. Now."

To Rest

"Two things, actually," she said. "First, please, could someone move Claire? Cover her or something."

Carter and Brass exchanged a glance. "Uh, Jake, do you have something...?"

"Yeah," replied Jake. "Yeah, here."

He stepped to the kitchen table, and rolled the tablecloth off it.

Held it out.

Jim, Brass, Tom, and Carter took the tablecloth. Unfolded it and lay it next to Claire.

They rolled Claire into it.

"I'm sorry," said Carter. "I said you'd be okay, Claire, but I was wrong. I'm sorry."

Jim squeezed his arm. "She did an amazing thing," he said. "We all were still staring at this crazy shit, but it was Claire that saw what was happening. It was Claire that moved first. As fucked up as she was, she moved, and saved the baby. That's a good thing."

He and Carter locked eyes for a moment, and then both looked away.

"Put her in here," said Jake, pointing toward one of the rooms. "There's a bed. It's a good place."

They all lifted her and carried her back.

One by one, they returned to the front room.

The floor was wet with blood and gore, and the thing that used to be Mark still lay twisted and destroyed.

"You don't get the good treatment," said Carter. "Fuck you, man."

Even Jim nodded at that.

Assume A Spherical Cow

For a moment, they all stared at the fragmented beast.

Jim spoke first. "You're right, Rose. This is a problem. All problems are solvable, one way or another. It's the first thing you learn – how to construct a basic management task."

"This isn't a management issue, Jim," she said.

He looked at her. "I can solve management issues, so, yes, if you want my help, then this is a management issue. Don't ask me to solve life-or-death issues. I can't *do* that. But I *can* do *this*. I *can* solve management issues."

"Well, then," said Jake. "Solve it."

Jim looked at all of them. "Okay," he said.

There's so much blood!

His head wasn't wrapped around that.

He nodded. Then nodded more forcefully.

Don't think about that. Think about the problem. Solve the problem. All problems have solutions, but if you try to ubermanage all the variables, you'll fuck yourself, so get rid of that. Get rid of the blood. Get rid of the woman. Get rid of it all. Focus on the problem. Solve the problem.

He nodded a third time. "Okay," he said. "Okay. So, what do we know?"

He looked at each of them. "C'mon, what do we know? What can we say about them?"

"They're not werewolves," said Tom. "Unless we're shooting silver bullets. I can't speak for anyone else here, but my bullets are normal. Assuming silver is the thing that kills werewolves. I don't know. Never shot a werewolf before." He paused. "As far as I know."

"Yeah," said Carter. "Ordinary bullets. Effective."

"Besides, it's not a full moon," said Rose. "Aren't werewolves supposed to come out at the full moon or something?"

"I heard that, yeah," said Carter. "Full moon."

166

Jake shook his head. "Jesus, people, what does it matter whether or not they're fuckin' werewolves?"

"It matters," said Jim. "It matters because if we think we know what they are and we aren't right, then we can fuck up. We start making assumptions and then we get surprised when they don't work that way, and then we die. So, let's not die. You asked me to solve this, so let's solve it."

"Fine," said Jake. "They're werewolves. Whatever."

"No, no, that doesn't help," said Jim. "I mean, sure, they might be, but what do we know about werewolves? Have you ever hunted them in the wild? I haven't. What I know of werewolves I got from the movies and last time I checked, the movies also tell me that midichlorians explain how Yoda can lift a spaceship with his hand, so let's not count on the movies to tell us what to do, okay?"

Carter started "So, what *do* we—?"

"We need a *functional* description," finished Jim. "Effects. Actions. Observed things."

"I've observed that I can shoot them and they fall down and stay dead," said Tom.

Jim nodded. "Like people. Check. What else?"

"Doesn't have to be a headshot, either," said Carter.

"Right, not zombies, check. They stay dead once we kill them. What else?"

"They're smart," said Rose.

Jim blinked at her. "How smart?"

"Smart," she said. "They distracted us at the front while they attacked in the rear."

Jim turned to Jake. "Are you sure that's what it was?"

Jake shrugged.

"Hey, Jim – I'm over here," said Rose.

"I know, I was just—"

"No, you weren't. You wanna crosscheck everybody, then crosscheck everybody, but if you only wanna crosscheck me, then we have a problem."

Jim shook his head. "I didn't mean anything. Can we just—"

"Do I have a gun?"

He stopped. "Well... yeah...?"

"Have I been shooting these fuckers?"

"Yeah, but I—"

"Then I'm part of the same team you're on, buddy, and that has nothing to do with my plumbing. So knock that shit off."

Jim stared at her. "Okay," he said. "Good point. Mea culpa. So, they're smart."

"And organized."

"Damn, that's so not good," said Jim.

"You're telling me," she replied.

"They have fingers," said Tom.

He kicked at the dead thing's front paws. A clenched hand unfolded, black skin on a humanlike hand. Long thin claws curved away where the nails had previously been human.

"People fingers."

"Damn," said Carter. "I never noticed that."

"Probably a good thing. Otherwise, you might have gotten nailed, too. This might be *your* hand we were looking at."

They stared at the hand.

"Do you think they could use them?" asked Jim. "You think they could open a car door or something?"

"What kind?" asked Carter.

"Why does that matter?" asked Jake.

"Some are easy, some are hard. Plymouths are a bitch on our fingers, but one of those flip-up types, even a dog could open one of those."

"Yeah, yeah," said Jim. "Volkswagens are the same way. Total pain in the ass to open."

"Only the earlier models," said Carter. "Didn't they switch that in the Eighties?"

"Not in the domestic models. You're thinking of—"

"*Why does it matter?*" shouted Jake. "There are no cars. No cars. Zero cars. All the cars are dead. We need something *useful*, not this circle jerk." He turned and walked away. "Fuck this," he grumbled, and stepped into the darkness of the back rooms.

For a second, no one spoke.

"They're infectious," said Tom. "Crazy-ass infectious."

Jim looked up. "You're a vet. You haven't seen anything at all like this?"

"No, you're not getting me – this shit is fast. I don't know what the hell it is, but not even a virus works that fast."

"What about snake venom? I heard that black mambas can kill you in, like, seconds."

"Venom, yeah, venom's nasty, but this is faster. Venom works fast because it has a very simple function. This is doing all kinds of other shit, and in less time. It's not venom. There's nothing like it that I know of. *Nothing* can do that to a man even in ordinary time, much less a few minutes."

Jim nodded. "Okay, infectious. Bite, claw, but not ordinary touch."

Tom nodded. "Through blood, then. Saliva, too. Heck, I don't even know what's under the nails or claws or whatever, but that does it, too."

"They're fast," said Carter.

"Not faster than dogs, though," said Jim.

"Not with those paws," added Tom. "Probably a lot slower." He kicked the front hand-paw. "If they were even as fast as dogs, they would have caught us in a couple of seconds, but they're not. This isn't made for speed. Not like a dog, and definitely not like a wolf."

"The rest of it looks like a wolf," said Jim.

"Yeah, I'll grant you that, except for the standing on two legs thing, which it's not good at anyway. It's like a wolf with human hands. That's nutty."

"They pack up," said Carter. "At least they seem to."

Jim nodded. "So maybe there's a pattern, or maybe there's a leader. That might be useful to know."

"Maybe that's what scared them off," said Carter. "Maybe we got their leader?"

"I doubt it," said Tom. "They moved like it was time to move. If there's a leader, it's still out there."

Jake stepped into the room, reloading his shotgun. His face was still a cloud of grim.

Erin spoke up. "They're more like people than wolves. No sense of smell."

"With a snout like that?" asked Tom.

"I'm telling you what I know. They can't see any better than us, hear any better than us, or smell any better than us. If they could, I'd be dead, so they can't."

"Maybe they weren't close enough," said Jim.

"You want a fucking hair sample? I could have reached down and grabbed one for you, if I hadn't been so busy trying to be invisible."

"Okay, okay, so they're not wolves in that respect. I think that means maybe they're as dumb as people can be. That would be nice."

"Hey," said Jake.

The others turned to him.

"I got a question." He turned to face Carter. "What's in that bag you got there?"

Something's In The Bag

Carter stared at him. "Nothing."

"My ass, nothing. I seen the way you two protect that bag. I seen the way you make magazines come out of it like you're Santa's Little Helper."

Carter glanced at Rose.

Rose shifted Sean ever-so-slightly.

"No, no, you look at *me,* not her."

Carter's head snapped back.

"I think we're all sitting around jerking each other off about what we know and what we don't know and what our resources are and what kind of fucking car they can open, and all I keep thinking about while I'm reloading is that goddamn bag of yours. So, what's in it?"

"There's nothing in it."

"It's under my roof. *What's in the goddamn bag, Carter?*"

Jim raised his hands. "Whoa, whoa, Jake, c'mon. What's going on?"

Jake rounded on him. "You want to know what your resources are, right?" He pointed at Carter's bag. "There's a resource for you right there. I have watched him pull magazines out of that bag like rabbits out of a hat, so as far as I'm concerned, that's a fucking resource, and as far as I'm concerned, seeing as how this is my house and my rules, that's a fucking resource I need to know about!"

"It's nothing," repeated Carter.

"If it's nothing," said Jake, turning back to him. "Then prove it. Show me."

Carter stared at him. "It's private," he said.

"Not here. Not now." He reached for the bag and Carter jumped back like he was bitten. "C'mon, Carter, what's in the bag?"

He reached again, and Carter swung the bag around behind him.

"Knock it off!"

Jake pressed. Carter backed away.

"I told you it's nothing. It's private."

"Show me, Carter."

"No!"

Carter was backed into a corner. Jake was right in front of his face.

They both fell silent.

Jake looked down.

Carter's shaking hand held a pistol pressed to Jake's belly.

Without tilting his head, Jake looked into Carter's eyes. When he spoke, his voice had switched back to the deadly-level he had used against Deedee.

"Your gun," he said. "It appears to have arranged itself to point at me."

Carter's eyes jerked. Not quite a full panic, but knocking on the door. "Please, don't."

Still quietly, still calmly, Jake said "Are you sure it's worth the trouble? Very, very sure?"

Dark Santa

Carter weighed his options.

Slumped.

"Okay."

The pistol lowered.

Carter stepped around Jake and headed for the kitchen table. It was still bare from when Jake pulled the tablecloth off.

Carter reached into his bag and brought out a rectangular package, plastic-surfaced, and the size of a small shoebox.

"There."

"I knew it," said Jake. "You brought drugs into my..." his voice trailed off as he examined the package.

The box was hard plastic. A small label on the end of the box, typed somewhere using an actual manual typewriter, read *ELIZABETH GREENE – MARCH 14, 2008. DO NOT DESTROY.*

"And don't forget this one, too," said Carter. He set another block on the table, identical to the first, except that the label read *ANTHONY GREENE – MARCH 14, 2008. DO NOT DESTROY.*

"...and this one, because you're going to want to see the whole set."

MELISSA GREENE – MARCH 14, 2008. DO NOT DESTROY.

Jake stared at the three boxes, confused.

"What are these...? 'Greene'...? Jefferson?"

Carter placed his hand on the one labeled *ELIZABETH.*

"His daughter."

ANTHONY

"His son."

MELISSA

"His wife."

He touched his own chest. "His other son."

Jake shook his head. "But... but Jefferson didn't *have* any kids. I've known him for nearly—"

"He never knew," said Carter. "Mom wanted it that way. Can't say as I blame her, the more I see how he lived down here. But I figured..." He passed a hand over the blocks. "...this changed everything. I figured it was time he knew, time he had a chance to learn something about a family he never knew he had. While I could still remember. While I still had the courage to talk with him. But, I guess I came just a little bit late, because apparently, my father was eaten by things-that-aren't-werewolves, and so now I have to figure out what to do with my dead family."

He leaned forward into Jake's face. Still in shock, Jake pulled back.

"So, yeah, it's personal. Very fucking personal."

Jake couldn't speak for a moment, and when he did, his voice was lower, more human, and less angry.

"I'm sorry. Oh god, I had no idea."

"I didn't say anything. I didn't think there would be a problem."

Jake shook his head. "I'm sorry, Carter. I was stupid. I thought you had guns in there, or drugs, or something."

Carter shrugged. "Sure. That too."

Coke Does Not Technically Add Life

He reached in and pulled out a different brick. This brick was smaller, wrapped in foil and clear plastic.

Dropped it on the desk.

"That is, how do the kids say it these days, our 'core business model.' Transport. So, I got lucky and Hatchet Valley is close to my delivery, so I figure hey, better late than never, so I'll bring along the family and plan for a proper reunion. But, instead of picking a day that would involve a lot of awkward social constructs, we arrived on Monster Day and we get to watch people be torn apart."

He tapped the drug block on the table.

"You want to spend the rest of your short and miserable life coked up? Be my guest, man. I doubt I'll get out of here alive, so might as well use it for good, huh? Go right ahead. Fuck it, I don't care, and after I tell him what happened, I'll bet my buyer wouldn't care either. I am, in fact, running on zero number of give-a-fucks today."

He turned to Rose.

"Honey, I'm quitting. Sorry we didn't get the last big score, but I'm quitting. Right now. No waiting."

She nodded once. "I'm okay with this plan."

Carter turned back to Jake.

"And I forgot that there *is* something useful here. Something you can use."

Carter tipped the bag and dumped the contents out onto the table. Several dozen cardboard boxes. Ammunition.

"Sorry it couldn't be more. Real sorry."

Jake picked up one of the boxes and squinted at it.

"What the hell are 'flechettes'?" he asked.

175

"Darts," Carter said. "Steel darts. Instead of bullets, you load these. They cut through anything and tear up meat something awful. They were so mean, the Army forbids using them. Twelve gauge. Fill your boots."

"Jesus, you were delivering these *here?*"

"Apparently, your neighbors aren't the white picket fence type, either. So..." Carter dropped the empty bag and placed his hands on his hips. "Are we done fucking around?"

Behind Rose's back, her revolver was half-drawn. She eased the hammer down, and slid the revolver back into place.

Sean wriggled in her arms.

She looked down, and unfolded the blanket that covered him.

Two thin furry arms reached out and clamped on her shoulders.

Hit Or Miss

With a shriek, Rose shoved Sean across the room. In any ordinary circumstances, a baby being hurled across a room is a horrible thing, but somehow, a baby that is covered in gray fur and squealing and thrashing and tearing its blanket open in shreds makes the experience less terrifying than one might think.

The Terrible Twos Come Early

Sean smacked into the wall and fell. His tiny gaunt body spun and tore the last bits of blanket fabric apart.

Tom raised his gun. "Oh, for fuck's sake," he said, squeezing off a round.

The shot missed, shattering a chunk of baseboard.

The tiny beast snarled and ran.

"Get it! Get it!" shouted Jim. He also fired, and missed.

The thing scampered behind the couch, shoving and pushing through the tiny gap.

Brass fired, and a section of the couch burst into a puffy white explosion of stuffing.

"Dammit!" shouted Jake. "Stop shooting my house!"

"Get the couch!" shouted Carter. He and Jim ran to either side of the couch, grabbed the arms.

"Don't let it get you," warned Jim. He wrapped his hands around an armrest and braced his legs. "Ready?"

Carter nodded.

Jim turned to Brass. "Ready?" he asked.

Brass took aim and nodded.

Jim turned back to Carter. "On three, okay? One... two... *three!*"

They yanked the couch from the wall.

There was nothing behind it.

"Flip the couch," shouted Jake. "*Flip the couch!*"

They rolled the couch forward, into the center of the room, and clinging to the bottom of it, spiderlike, was the creature that used to be Sean.

Just as it leaped, Brass fired, missing.

Tom fired, also missing.

It ran toward Carter, who fired, but a tiny snarling pseudo-werewolf is enough to mess up anyone's aim, and Carter also missed. It was a close enough shot, however, to freak the thing out, because it bounced in another direction.

It ran under tables, it ran around posts, it even crabbed across the body of the thing that had been its own father. Every time it came close to someone, they shot at it or kicked at it, and it backed away.

At this point, the most fatal gunshot wounds were inflicted to the house's baseboards.

Brass fired four rounds at it in rapid succession, each one closer. The last must have gotten its attention, because it turned and jumped at Brass.

Full swing, Jake's boot caught the thing in its exposed ribcage. It was a solid connection, and the Sean beast was flung across the room, where it struck the already shredded remains of a few curtains.

For a fraction of a second, it tried to untangle its claws from the lace, but before it could, a silver needle flashed through the air, and the hilt of a throwing knife sprouted from the thing's face.

It dropped to the floor, dead as shit.

There was a moment of shock, then Jake turned.

Erin rolled her pants leg back down over the obvious scabbard. She looked up, and shrugged.

"Letter opener," she said.

In three angry steps, Tom stood above the beast, which still lay on the ground, mewling and clawing at its face.

"You little bastard," he muttered and shot it.

Everyone stopped and stared at the chunked remains that used to be a tiny werewolf that used to be a tiny baby.

Almost everyone.

"Carter," said Rose.

Family Business

She sat on her knees, swaying back and forth.

The two thin scratches on her shoulders were dark purple, inflamed, pulsing.

"No, no, no..." murmured Carter as he jumped to her, kneeling beside her. He took her shoulders in his hands and she looked at him, smiling.

"Baby, I been thinking about it," she said. Her voice sounded tired. More tired than he had ever heard it.

"Whatcha been thinking about?"

"I think we can get out of the smuggling business."

Carter nodded at her. "Yeah, I think that's a good idea, too. I mean, look where it got us."

"Yeah, a bad end. Sorry."

"Don't be sorry. It was my choice, too."

"I know, but I'm sorry I contributed to it."

"Don't be. Don't be at all. Look, Rose. Rose?" She looked at him. "I agree completely. I think we should quit. I was ready a few minutes ago and now I think we can make it official."

She nodded. "The money's nice. I know that's been a big thing. But you're not happy, baby, and that matters a lot to me. It always has, but I think you need to hear it now. I want you to be happy. If you aren't happy, then why do it, right? Why?"

"No reason at all," he said.

"I'm okay with taking a loss on this one. Let's chalk it up to a bad deal and walk away. I want you to be happy."

Carter's eyes were wet. "I'll be happy. I swear. I'll be happy."

Rose wobbled. The skin of her shoulders turned dark. Thin trails wormed their way through her neck and down her shoulders into her arms.

Tom drew. "She's gonna change," he said.

In the history of their lives together, Rose and Carter had disagreed on many things. One of the things they often disagreed on was when deadly force was appropriate and necessary. Usually, it wasn't much of an issue, so the discussion remained in the realm of the hypothetical. Usually.

Rose and Carter both drew and Tom found himself staring down the barrels of Rose's revolver and Carter's automatic. They each cocked at the same instant.

"*BACK OFF!*" they both shouted.

Tom backed off. Way off.

Rose panted, but managed to speak. "This is something you don't *get* to fix, doc." Her eyes slipped closed and she swayed. Then she jerked back awake.

She handed her revolver to Carter, butt-first.

"You do it," she said.

"But—" he started to say, and stopped when he looked into her eyes.

Carter sighed, resigned.

He looked at the two guns in his hands. "Yours or mine?" he asked.

"It doesn't matter, baby, I know you'll do the right thing no matter which you use."

He shook his head.

She reached out and touched his arm. The skin on her forearm was already shifting, wrinkling, folding and unfolding, darkening.

"It's okay," she said. "You have to. It's a good thing."

She touched his cheek.

Pulled him toward her.

Kissed him.

Convulsed.

Bent and panting, she whispered "Hurry."

Carter scrambled to his feet.

Stepped back.

Aimed.

"I love you," he said. "I love you so much."

"Damn right you do, baby." She looked up and the darkness had spread across her face. One eye swirled iridescent black. "Love you, too."

Her voice guttered out on the last word.

Carter fired twice.

Rose fell.

The only sound was his panting.

Tom started to move, but Jake motioned him to remain where he was.

Carter dropped the revolver to the floor.

He turned and looked at the faces around him, the horror of his own work reflected in their eyes.

"Excuse me," he said, and stepped out of the room.

Carnage

Jim, Brass, Tom, Jake, and Erin stared at each other, and stared at the carnage in the room.

Finally, Jake stepped away. He didn't say anything, didn't excuse himself, didn't even look at anyone else. He stepped away and followed Carter into the dark recesses of the cabin's rooms.

"Jesus," said Jim.

Shock The Monkey

Erin looked up. "We need electricity," she said.

"What?" asked Jim.

"Electricity. We need it. They'll attack again, and it was the electricity that made them stop. So, we need to get the lights back on. We need power. If we can get the power back..."

"...then we can shock the fuckin' monkey again," said Tom. "Nice."

Jim nodded. "Okay, so, yeah. We need to find the breakers."

"Probably fuses in a house this old," said Tom.

"Attic?" asked Jim.

"Maybe an attic," said Tom. "I would expect an attic or a basement."

"I saw stairs earlier," said Erin. "Stairs going down."

"That sounds promising," said Tom.

Heavy Petting

The basement was a dark place that reeked of thick dirt, moist mold, and a little vinegar.

A muffled voice.

A rattling of a latch.

A creak of a wooden door.

Wan light split the darkness.

"See, I wasn't lying," whispered Erin.

Erin, Tom, Brass, and Jim stepped down the rickety handmade wooden steps until all three stood on the ground.

The basement was large, and hand dug, but neatly hand dug.

"You really think there's a fuse box down there?" asked Jim.

"That's where I would put it," said Tom.

"How are we going to find it?"

"We spread out, look for a gray box on the wall or on a post. That's the simplest—"

They stepped past a rack of digging tools – picks, shovels, hoes, mattocks, and at least one thing that looked to Erin like it was designed exclusively to lop off heads. She touched the edge of the blade and it felt sharp.

Next to that was a wooden crate, four feet to a side. A tied canvas tarp covered it.

A metal clanking stopped Tom. He listened, which good because everyone else was straining to listen, but failed at being quiet enough.

More clanking. Chain on concrete.

A long set of shelves bisected the basement, filled with cans and bottles and boxes. Jim played a penlight over the labels. Canned food, dried food, and more food. "You could live in this basement," he muttered.

"Wouldn't be fun, though," replied Tom.

Another clank.

They looked at each other.

The shelves blocked their view into the other part of the basement, the place where the sound was coming from.

The four of them slipped around the corner.

At the edge of the shelves, the room opened up.

They turned the corner.

Before anyone recognized the deep rumbling growl as even a real sound, the great shaggy beast leaped.

Vows

In midair, the thing stopped short, jerked by a heavy metal chain. It fell to the ground, scrabbled to its feet and snarled at them, lunging against the chain.

Around its body, a rudimentary harness had been constructed of sections of half-inch chain, padlocked in several places to sew it up. In two places, the harness had been locked to a connector chain that led to the wall. In three places on the wall, the chain was also padlocked.

It strained at the harness, staring at them with shining, hungry eyes.

Tom spoke in a low, incredulous voice. "You have *got* to be fucking kidding me. Farmer John has a fucking dog problem?"

Brass drew his gun. Jim and Tom followed suit.

In the darkness past the beast, there was another sound. It was the sound of a shotgun being cocked.

"I would appreciate it if you put those down," said Jake. "I would hate to think of what would happen if you hurt anything important."

"Jake?" asked Erin. "Where are you?"

Jake sighed. "I'm where the other precious things are kept. The things I need to survive. So, if you please, step away from her."

"Her?" asked Jim.

Erin looked into the beast's eyes again, this time more deeply. "His wife," she said.

They lowered their guns.

The thing paced at the end of the chain. Its eyes never left the four intruders.

"She begged me, too," said Jake. "Just like your gal upstairs. She begged me to kill her, to make the pain stop, and to keep her from becoming this. But I couldn't. I couldn't."

He crouched down and the creature spun and jumped, seeing a chance.

Once again, the chain yanked it to the ground inches away from where Jake sat.

Frustrated, it snapped twice at him, and then sat back, staring. Hungry.

"I thought maybe it was like in the movies," said Jake. "I thought maybe once the sunlight came, she would change back and things would be fine. Maybe, you know, maybe we could work something out. This is a sturdy basement, the chain's strong, and the tranquilizer works."

"Nice," said Tom. "I was wondering how you caught her."

"I'm not saying it was easy, mind you, but the tranks helped. They let me build a harness for her."

Erin shook her head. "I'm sorry, Jake."

"For what? You didn't do anything."

"No, not for this. For the sunlight thing. Sunlight won't matter. I know it won't help."

The Problem With Sunlight

Erin sighed. "They tore my father apart. He dragged himself, trying to get into the camper, and he went right through the sunlight. He was in the sunlight and they were in the sunlight and they didn't change back. They just tore him apart."

"You said you were asleep," said Jim.

"I wasn't asleep. Who can sleep through that? Who can sleep through three people screaming while they're being ripped apart? I wasn't asleep. I was behind the door. I locked it and I hid, hoping they would never know I was there. Hoping they would leave after killing three of us. Hoping they wouldn't think to look inside the RV."

"It sounds like there was nothing you could—" Tom started to say.

"Don't you think I know that?" asked Erin. "Don't you think I've redone the past six hours of my life a few dozen times already. I *know* there was nothing I could do. But it doesn't matter. I tell myself I acted smart. I tell myself that there was nothing I could have done to help them, and that being alive is better than being not alive – or being one of those things. But it doesn't matter. I was scared. I was scared and I locked the door and no one could get in. Not even my own father, who was a decent guy even when I was being a total bitch. That's love. And I locked him out and they fucking tore him apart."

The room was silent. Even the great wolf stopped pacing and watched Erin.

"I stayed there, staring at his body, after they left. In the sunlight. I saw him shift and change. In the sunlight. I saw him stand back as one of those things. In the sunlight. And then he ran away to join them, and I was left alone."

Jake nodded.

"I thought I wanted to be left alone," she continued. "But as with so many things in life, apparently, once we have it, we realize that it includes a bucket of shit we never expected."

She turned to Jake.

189

"So, I'm sorry, Jake, but sunlight will not help her. I wish I could say otherwise. I do. I'm so sorry."

Jake stared hard at this woman he mistook for a girl mere moments earlier.

"So..." said Tom. "What are we going to do about *her?* We can't leave her down here."

In the dim shafts of light cast through airborne dust, Jake's eyes glittered.

Erin saw this, and she understood.

"Nothing," she said.

"What?!" asked Jim.

Erin's eyes never left Jake's eyes. "We're not going to do anything," she said. She turned to face Jim. "We're going to go back upstairs. Jake can fix the fuses on his own. There's nothing down here that concerns us."

Jim was confused, Tom's eyes bounced from Erin to the wolf creature, and Brass watched it all.

Erin stared them down.

"Yeah, I guess you're right," said Tom. "Time to go back upstairs and get ready to make shit happen."

He pulled Jim out of the hypnosis and back toward the stairs. Brass followed.

With one last glance toward the dark place that held Jake, Erin turned to join them.

Watchers

Just beyond the edge of the trees, they watched the cabin. There were fewer of them, but still more than enough to follow the blood song and to spread. First, though, finish this.

Listeners

Erin glanced out the dark window. She saw nothing, but she knew they were out there. She knew they were watching and waiting. She knew something was coming.

"We should do something," said Jim.

She looked at him. He looked troubled. More troubled than he looked before. How strange. *All these people dead and you weather that,* she thought, *but this one man and his wife troubles you so much?*

Tom glanced at her. *He expects me to answer.*

That makes sense. I did something down there. I did something Jim hasn't done yet. I took over. Jesus, I took over and it was that simple.

"We did," she said. "We did exactly what we needed to do."

"No," said Jim. "I mean we—"

A shot rang out from the basement.

A broken howling scream followed.

Another shot rang out.

Then there was silence.

Three seconds later, there was not.

Mourners

They knew what happened. In a way that made no sense to any human being, they knew that one of their own had died. Not in battle, not in conflict, but in some other strange soul-wrenching way.

One of theirs had died in love.

They howled.

The End Of The Song

The cabin's lights flickered, then switched on.

Power was restored.

Thirty seconds later, Jake stepped into the room, his shoulders slumped. He looked at no one.

No one spoke to him.

The howling outside was a constant song, thick and warbling. It wasn't a song of men, nor was it a song of wolves. It was an alien song that used their voices and used their hearts. It was a song of loss, a song of confusion, a song of senselessness and violence.

Jake righted the couch. Set the end table next to it.

Sat down.

Erin sat down next to the old man. She said nothing. Made no movement, no offer, no sound. Just sat by him.

There was nothing to say.

And then the howling stopped.

Locked In, Locked Out, Locked Up

The front door shuddered from impact. Angry howls tore through the air.

More window glass crashed as toothy faces jammed through.

Everybody jumped up, but it was Brass who acted first. It was Brass who stepped to the front windows, to the section of the bars that were most bent, who drew his pistol, and who perforated the furred doglike face poking through.

Jake stood up. Looked around. "Where's Carter?"

Jim joined Brass at the window, firing at faces and figures as they passed by, or as they stopped to attack a new weakness.

"Carter!"

From the back of the house, a shot rang out.

Jake looked that way. Jim and Brass looked at each other.

Erin knew what they were thinking. She was also thinking it. *Please be shooting werewolves,* she begged the Universe.

A second shot rang out.

Despite the fact that her world was all death and teeth these days, Erin sighed a huge sigh of relief.

The door shook from another impact. The frame rattled.

Jim jumped away from his place at the window and stared at the door.

It shook again.

Another face rammed through the bars of the window, but Jim didn't turn. He stared at the door.

Jake noticed, and turned enough to cover both spots. He fired and with a yelp, the thing fell away.

"Jim, can you go see what happened?" he asked.

Jim turned to Jake. He tried to speak, but his mouth moved without making a sound. His face grew pale.

Jake turned to Brass. "Brass!"

Brass stopped firing and looked over.

"Can you go see what's happening back there? I can cover here."

Brass glanced from Jake to Jim. For a brief moment, he assessed his friend, then nodded back at Jake.

Tom moved to take Brass's place. Aimed and fired.

Another wolf fell.

Three more shots rang out, and Carter's voice followed: "I need a hand! They're at the back door!"

Tom and Jake exchanged a glance.

"I'll go," said Erin.

She scooped up Rose's revolver, grabbed some boxes from the table, and tugged at Brass's sleeve.

"Hey," said Jake.

Erin stopped.

"You know what you're doing with that thing?"

Erin eyed the revolver, then looked back at Jake. "I won't put my eye out," she said.

She and Brass disappeared into the dark hallway.

The Eye Of The Storm

A whirlpool of gray fur and flesh, spiraled around the cabin. First the front, a run against the door, then the barred windows, a run against those in hopes of bending them further, then a run around to the back, tearing at the small windows en route, and then crashing against the bars of the back door.

Then back to the front.

Every one of them was doing this.

This was the plan that Streak thought would work. This was how they would pry apart the walls of the cabin and reach the insides.

In part of Streak's distant memory, he saw the word that described this. He saw it as his man-part had seen it, but now he couldn't have said it to save his life. He knew, though, what it meant, and this was his plan.

The word was "maelstrom."

Regular Checkups

Erin and Brass stumbled though the dark hallway.

She stopped. "Hey," she said.

Brass stopped.

"You okay?" she asked.

"I'm okay."

"Really? Because suddenly I'm not sure you're okay. Suddenly I'm thinking you might have half a mind still out there on Jim."

Brass blinked at her.

"The doc'll fix him," she said. "One way or another. You know the doc. He's no slouch. He'll fix Jim, right?"

"Yeah. Yeah, he'll fix him."

"Good. I need you to believe this, Brass, so you can be with *us*. One hundred percent with us. I need you to be putting bullets in heads, to be shooting these things. Not worrying about Jim."

Three more shots rang out.

Carter's voice was louder, around the corner. "Anybody? *Hey!*"

Brass straightens up. "One hundred percent," he said.

Erin nodded once, then yelled back "On our way!"

They ran.

Honey

Like wasps attacking a honeybee nest, gray wolf things crowded around the back door.

Their growls merged into a continuous ululation.

The flashing lights from within the back door signaled death, but the pack knew there were so many lights, so many stings, and then there would be no more lights and no more stings.

Only sweet, hot honey.

Triple-X

Carter's ammo supply was low, but he was going to keep firing until there was none, because that was how one handled an infestation of whatever the fuck these were. He was sure that although this particular scenario was never covered in firearms training career, had it been an option, his instructor would have recommended this exact strategy. So far, it had proven rather effective, although the lack of an infinite supply of bullets was going to become problematic.

The back door bars were bending and starting to break. He would shoot each one of the things that touched the door, and a lot of times, he managed to hit, but the constant stream of beasts never stopped. No one single one would stick around long enough. They would run up, smash into things, and then run off.

Unfortunately, this was proving to be an effective tactic.

At his side, he heard a loud snarl. And close!

He spun.

One of the things was already halfway through the tiny side window. Another one almost pushed though the metal grating on the back door. He was already pointed that way, so he shot it first.

The shot sounded weird, though, like a double-shot.

He turned to dispatch the bastard at the small window, only to see spurting meat hanging there. It was dead *and* it was being a fine block.

Carter looked behind him.

Brass's gun still smoked, and behind him, Erin stepped up with...

Why her gun? Why hers? Isn't it right that it and she retire at the same time? No, no, that's not right and you know it. If Rose had thought of it, she would have done it herself.

Erin aimed and fired and Carter turned to see what she hit.

The top half of a wolf was gone.

200

That's right, baby, said the voice in his head. *She's perfect. It's perfect for her. Let her do the good work she's doing.*

"Glad you made it!" he said. "I'm almost out."

Erin tossed him a box of flechettes. "Try these," she said. "I hear they're good for what ails you."

Brass slid next to him as he reloaded, and fired again at the back door.

More yelps.

ICU

Erin watched the two men clear away the back door.

Out the corner of her eye, she saw something move past the tiny window.

She watched as the headless corpse was pulled away from the outside.

She aimed.

The revolver kicked. She knew intellectually it kicked, but feeling it was a whole different matter. She knew working it was a matter of taking aim, firing, and recovering for a second. But as long as she knew that, she thought it would be okay.

Then she remembered how Rose used it, how Rose took aim, even while other people were shooting. And she remembered how Rose never missed.

That's the way to do it, she thought. Although that voice didn't quite feel like *her* voice. And the revolver felt more natural than it did a few minutes earlier when she picked it up. And she was a lot calmer now than she was when she arrived at the back door.

The body fell from the window and another head poked up.

She fired and it vanished in a spray.

She kept staring, because...

...because there's something out there. Something important.

She stepped closer to the window, her eyes searching the darkness.

And then, a patch of dark against the dark, deep in the dark, but she saw it.

She saw him.

The Abyss Gazes Back

Streak watched the whirlpool of teeth and claw around the cabin. He watched the bursts of light, and felt sad when each of his own fell, but he knew it was it was all going to change soon.

Wait.

What was that?

His hackles rose. Something wasn't right. Something was coming that was very, very wrong. He felt it like a huge stone rolling toward him, slowly but gathering speed.

"My Hand is Steady, My Eyes Keen."

She raised the revolver. She could see the one wolf, in the distance, as clear as day.

All the sounds of gunfire fell away. All the smells of fire and blood fell away.

There was her and there was him.

She knew this was the one. The one that mattered.

She felt the wood of the revolver in her hands, and it felt like an old friend. An old friend who wanted to help. An old friend who was a part of her body, a part of her mind, and a part of her will.

She sighted along the barrel, brought the bead right in line.

...a little bit up, just a little...

Her breathing slowed. She felt her heartbeat. And then, she squeezed the trigger.

The instant she squeezed the trigger, she knew where the bullet would fly. She knew it would slip out the window, straight and true. She knew it would cross the yard cleanly. She knew it would fly into this fiend, and burst into a dozen fragments. She knew it would tear the entire top half of the creature to pieces. She knew that this was the perfect moment.

The voice inside her knew this. The cold angry voice. The vengeful voice. The voice that threw itself into the bullet, that promised to ride the tiny spinning piece of metal all the way until it had destroyed the mind that drove the beasts.

Time stretched.

She felt the voice fall into the bullet as it moved out of the barrel. She saw the flash at the muzzle, the tiny sparks of burnt powder.

She saw the bullet.

And then she saw the face.

The face of the thing that had jumped into the window. The gray stupid face of one of the many beasts circling the cabin. The gray stupid face that had through sheer bad luck jumped past the window the instant she had squeezed the trigger.

The voice cried out in frustration, but it was small and far away.

The bullet struck the wolf's face.

The bullet destroyed itself in the meat, and split the wolf thing's head wide open.

And there it stopped.

It did not continue through the yard. It did not burrow into the distant wolf's head like it was supposed to.

It hit a wolf in the middle and it killed that wolf, but the thing that was not a bullet, that held her arm steady, that showed her how to breathe, and that rode with the bullet...

That thing was also gone.

Once again, she was alone.

She stared at the distant creature, who also stared back at her. It was majestic and terrifying.

"*Bad dog!*" she screamed. "*Bad, bad dog!*"

It ran down from the hill and disappeared into the dark.

Carpet

The ground in front of the cabin was littered with gray corpses. Most lay dead. A few lay snapping at their wounds, bleeding out, and soon to die.

Others ran over them, many ran on top.

There was no respect for the dead.

The dead were meat.

Heads I Lose

Jake was a machine. Aim, fire. Aim, fire. Aim, fire. Reload.

Tom was also holding his own. Aim, fire. Aim, fire.

They had stopped firing at every face appearing, preferring to wait until a wolf had bitten down on something. A bar, a curtain rod, glass, whatever. That made it still for half a second and in that half a second, it died.

Jim was not doing well. Jim was, in fact, doing poorly.

His eyes jumped from creature to creature, but his arm wouldn't move, his hand wouldn't fire. He twitched.

"Jim," shouted Jake. "C'mon, snap out of it. We need you, man!"

Jim turned and looked at Jake and then Jake realized what had happened.

He's shell-shocked.

Jake had heard of shellshock before – who hadn't – but never seen it in person. Never seen it lock a man down and away from the world.

"Tom?"

Tom looked at Jake, then followed his eyes to Jim. Shook his head. "We'll deal with it later," he said.

Tom fired and another creature fell back with a scream.

Jake fired.

"He's in the way," said Jim.

Tom nodded. "Jim!" he shouted. "Move away from the window. Jim, come here!"

Jim turned at the sound of his own name, confused by the request.

"Goddammit, get over here *now!*"

A light of understanding went off in Jim's head and he took a step away from the window.

A great black paw reached in and wrapped itself around Jim's neck.

He screamed, clawing at it. His gun clattered to the floor and he fell backwards against the ruined metal mesh.

It pulled him harder against the bars, but his body wouldn't go. His arms beat at the paw.

He kept screaming.

Jake aimed, but there was nothing to hit except the arm stretched around Jim's neck. Tom ran to the other side of the window, hoping to hit whatever it was from the side.

Jim's screams rose in pitch. His face purpled.

His head bent backwards.

"*Jim!*" screamed Jake. He couldn't see a clear thing to shoot at. He couldn't see anything.

"Fuck!" said Tom. He fired into the darkness, at the hard angle, hoping to miss Jim and hit the thing that was—

Jim's scream whipped into a shriek and then stopped.

Like giant knuckles cracking, his neck broke backwards.

And then his head was gone, torn off.

His body fell back into the room, blood pulsing from his neck.

"Fuckfuckfuckfuck!" shouted Tom. His gun was a blur and shots rang out so close together that it was a single sound.

Jake leaned in also, firing at anything that moved, no matter how far it was away. *Fuck conservation of ammo.*

Between Jake and Tom, more than twenty beasts died in a matter of seconds, and the rest felt it.

The wolves outside howled a howl of pain, a rippling cry that crossed from the front to the back.

Shreds

As Carter watched, the attack stopped. The howling things fell back and vanished into the trees.

Not entirely, though. He aimed and fired off one last shot. A wolf, invisible in the distance, fell.

At the same moment, he heard Brass and Erin also fire last shots.

Satisfyingly, screaming from the outside accompanied those shots.

"We couldn't have scared them off," said Carter.

"I'll take what I can get," said Erin.

Carter stepped to the doorway. Poked it with the toe of his shoe. Slabs of wood fell off, and chunks littered the ground.

"This place is coming apart," he said.

Echoes Again

Outside, the howling continued.

Words Sometimes Fail

Tom and Jake stared at each other. Between them, on the floor, lay Jim's body.

There were no words for this, no words for a man who was in such pain and confusion, but who was now free of that.

Each of them tried to speak, but stopped before words came out, because they each knew that before the words even came out, that the words weren't going to work.

Shift Change

"What happened?" asked Erin as she ran in.

She stopped short as soon as she saw the room.

As soon as she saw Jim.

Brass and Carter each nearly collided with her.

Brass's eyes locked on Jim.

Carter ran a hand through his hair. "Aw... Aw, man," he said in a low voice.

Brass stepped past everyone to Jim's side. Knelt down.

Jake knelt down across the body from Brass. "I'm sorry," he said.

Brass ignored him.

Erin watched Brass change. She watched him comprehend what was going on.

She watched him deflate.

She stepped up behind him. Waited.

Everyone waited.

Brass turned to her. There were no tears in his eyes. There was an emptiness. A place where there used to be dancing life of one sort or another.

Erin knew this emptiness.

She knelt down next to him. He dwarfed her, but his time, he had become so small, so shrunken, that they were the same size. The size of loss.

She spoke to him, softly.

"It's okay," she said. "It's okay to do this. I understand. God, I wish I didn't, but I understand."

He blinked at her.

She reached out, resting a hand on his arm. Not moving or shaking or squeezing, just resting a hand. Letting him know that there were other people in the world. People who knew how it felt.

"But we have to do it later," she said. "Right now, we need other things to happen. Right now, we need all of us to be functioning. We need to survive. We can do this later, I promise, but right now, we need you."

He didn't move. She cast about for a moment, and then realized what he needed.

It's what I needed, she thought.

"Everybody needs somebody," she said. "We need you. *I* need you."

Brass closed his eyes and took a deep breath.

Opened his eyes.

"Later?" he asked.

"I promise."

He nodded.

He looked once more at Jim's body, then stood up.

Erin stood up next to him.

"You're the boss," he said.

Going To Ground

The five of them stood, surrounded by glass and debris, surrounded by blood, surrounded by expended shells, surrounded by the dead.

Carter shook his head. "We can't handle another attack," he said.

He looked to Jake. "Please don't get me wrong," he said. "I deeply appreciate that you built this like a fucking fort, but who knew *this* would happen?"

Jake shrugged. "We can maybe hide in the bolthole," he said. "It's small, but it might work."

Erin shook her head. "I don't think that's an option anymore," she said. "They're too smart for that."

"What do you suggest?" asked Carter.

"I think we have to get out of here," said Erin. "I think we have to leave."

Jake slumped into a chair. Rested his head on his hand. "Where do you think we're going to go, girl genius?" he asked. "Hatchet Valley is a dead-end, right where you're standing. Cliff, cliff, cliff, and a road full of teeth. This I why I live here, so that assholes can only come from one side, and so few actually do. This is why you're here, too. In this valley, you're either dead or you're in my house."

Erin closed her eyes and shook her head, thinking. "No, no," she said. "I remember something. Something someone said, or something I saw... *Wait* – I remember! What's with all the digging gear I saw in the basement? Those weren't for gardens, they were more serious. Where have you been digging?"

Jake's eyes lit up. "The mine!" he said. "Yes, that might work. It's a helluva climb, but it might work." He pointed a finger at her. "I take back my sarcasm – you *are* a genius!"

"You said it was close?" asked Tom.

"Yeah," said Jake. "Close, but an uphill climb. Sorry, that's gonna be rough if we're being chased."

"We can hide in there?" asked Carter.

"It's not deep," said Jake. "About a hundred yards, then loops back. I suppose it's possible we could hide in there, and because it has a narrow mouth, we could defend it better."

Erin was staring at Jake. Something else was nibbling on her brain, trying to worm its way from a distant memory to the We Need To Review This Right Away file in her mind.

"Good thing you hadn't closed it," said Tom.

Jake shrugged and nodded.

"Jake," said Erin. "Can you tell me how you were thinking of closing the mine? What were you planning to do?"

End Of The Rainbow

In the dark basement, the door creaked open again, allowing a widening sliver of light into the room.

Erin stepped down and walked to the covered crate. With her throwing knife, she sliced through the tarp cord and unspooled it enough to pull the tarp away from the crate.

The top of the crate was missing.

She looked inside.

Her eyes grew wide and a wash of hope blew through her.

"Smash the fuckin' state, man," she whispered.

The crate was packed with row upon row of smaller crates. The smallest ones had "detonators" stenciled on the side. The larger ones had "dynamite" stenciled on the side.

"You find it?" asked Jake from upstairs.

Erin pulled herself away from the display, from the pure shock of being this close to that much explosive.

She turned to the open door, and she couldn't help but grin as she spoke. "You were thinking about being a very bad man, weren't you?"

"It's purely for home defense, of course," said Jake.

The Setup Comes Before The Punchline

The vests were works of art. While everyone else had a certain nervousness working with explosives, Brass had proven himself not only a clever engineer, but a clever engineer with a well-earned name.

Dynamite sticks formed a series of ribs across the front of each pack, and the chestpiece was a single small cardboard box, tape-wrapped into something magical and deadly. From each stick of dynamite, a detonator fuse led to the chestpiece.

Erin picked hers up and wrapped it over her shoulders. "Lighter than I thought," she said.

"This is nuts," said Carter. "I admit there's a kind of maniacal method to it, but seriously, are we going to walk around wearing these things? It's a suicide bomber's wet dream."

Erin eyed him. "We gotta run," she said. "In less than half an hour, I guarantee you that this is not going to be a happy place, so if you stick around, you're going to also be unhappy. On the other hand, we're going to be running, and doing our best to pop every puppy that gets close."

Tom shouldered his pack. "I can work with this," he said.

Jake came in from the back room.

"You get it all sealed up?" asked Erin.

"The bolt-hole is bolted," he said. "I hope it stays bolted after all the fun happens, but it's as battened down as I can batten anything with short notice."

He noticed the packs on the floor and whistled in appreciation. "Those look real nice," he said.

Carter shook his head and sighed.

While Jake pulled his pack on, Brass came from the basement, carrying a box. It was terrifying to see how much solid mass that man could carry in an almost casual fashion – the box looked heavy. He set it on the floor and opened it up.

"I made a few of these from our leftovers," he said. He lifted a firecracker-like pack of dynamite. The fuses were all connected to a single box, also duct-taped together.

"Those look like fun," muttered Carter. "How do we use them?"

"They work the same way the backpacks work. All the fuses go into a box. They share a little snapping flint igniter thing." Brass nodded at Jake. "I don't know what they're called."

Jake shrugged. "I don't either. I found them online. Thought they might be handy. You know, for home defense."

"They're handy," said Brass. "When you pull a stick out of the bunch, or out of your backpack, it lights the fuse. You want to throw it."

"How much time do the fuses take?" asked Erin.

"You want to throw it fast," said Brass. "This is kinda crappy fuse. Throw it as soon as you pull it."

"What if it's not lit?" asked Carter.

"Throw it anyway. You might get lucky." Brass paused for a moment. "Actually, if you pull it and it's not lit, then I suggest you throw the whole string."

"Why the whole string?" asked Tom.

"The igniter in the box is shared. The way it's supposed to work is that as you pull the fuse out, it spins the flint and lights the fuse, but if the fuse stays in the box, it'll ignite all the other fuses in the box. That would be very bad. So, if it doesn't come out lit, then throw the whole thing. Nothing might happen and you're still in one piece, or something might happen and you're still in one piece."

He handed out strings to each person. "I had enough to make a string for each of us."

"The same goes for the packs, right?" asked Jake. "If they don't light, throw the whole pack?"

"Yeah. Sorry, I should have said that," said Brass.

In a few minutes, each of the five was wearing a pack and carrying a string.

"Time for phase two," said Jake.

Erin nodded.

"Wait – there's a phase two?" asked Carter.

Erin patted him on the shoulder. "You know how you thought this was the crazy part?" she asked.

"Yeah," he said, but he sounded doubtful.

"Phase two is the crazy part."

"What do we have to do for phase two?"

"You, nothing. Phase two is all me. You're going to help with phase three, though, right now, before we execute phase four."

"I've kinda lost track of which phase is which," said Carter.

"The phase you gotta worry about is phase five," said Tom.

"What's phase five?"

"Run like hell. Blow up anything with four legs that comes close."

Phase Two

The front porch was quiet. In the distance, the bushes rustled as gray shapes passed through them.

The door creaked open.

Erin stepped out.

"I hate phase two already," she muttered. "I hate it like I hate garbage disposals and wood chippers. Phase two is the worst idea I've ever had."

She stomped on the porch wood and the sound echoed out into the dark.

She heard growling.

She took a deep breath. *Don't hyperventilate, take a deep breath. And make it sound good, not like a little girl.*

She didn't shout often, so she tried to keep her voice pitched low.

"Yo, *bitches!*"

Let's add insult to injury.

She howled.

She tried to make it sound like the howls she had heard outside.

Not bad, she thought. *I mean, not bad in a holy-shit-I-might-get-their-attention kind of way, which is not bad in a very-bad kind of way.*

They melted out of the distance, out of the woods, out of the hedges and bushes behind the cars. They came from the dark and from within the thin fog that had settled in. They walked on all fours.

They stared at Erin.

The air rumbled.

She howled again.

More shapes drifted toward her from the right of the cabin. Some came from the left of the cabin.

She tried counting, but any number over ten translated to "shit," "holy shit," "oh god," "jesus," and "we're gonna die," so she stopped counting. Instead, she watched for the ends.

All the creatures stopped a certain distance away, about twenty feet.

Good doggies, she thought.

She watched.

The group from the right side of the house thinned out and stopped.

Then the group from the left side of the house thinned out and stopped.

She looked across a yard filled with gray bitey death.

"Please be all of you," she muttered. "Please-oh-please-oh-please..."

Then she saw him.

The one with the streak across his face.

He was at the end of the group that came around from the left. The others lay down...

...like a dog right at the edge of the kitchen...

...but they all watched this one.

The cabin door was three feet behind her. Everywhere she looked, there were hungry eyes watching her. Hungry eyes in faces filled with teeth on furry meat machines that crept, inch-by-inch closer and closer.

They're waiting for you to give the command, she thought, looking at the streaky one. *You're their boss. They're your pack.*

She pointed at the pack leader and in a clear voice, said "I see you, motherfucker. I *see* you."

He growled.

The air throbbed with the growling of animal throats.

"Allllmost," she said. "Why did I think this was a good idea. This is not a good idea. Not a good idea at all. I hate the whole phase two idea."

The wolves paused ten feet away, but she could tell they wanted to jump.

She looked at the group. No stragglers. No new ones coming from the sides, or the back. Not even any close to the bushes – everybody was creeping closer and closer to the delicious ambulatory breakfast on the porch.

No self-deprecation, she thought. *Major life lesson – no being self-deprecating when facing down a pack of werewolves.*

221

This might be them all, she thought. *Okay, let's see how well I can play with those perky little ears of yours.*

She screamed.

She screamed as loud as she could and as shrill as she could.

It wasn't one of those glass-shattering screams, but it was loud in the growl-filled pseudo-silence.

There is no animal on Earth that a loud noise can't startle, including people. It stands to reason, therefore, that things which looked like wolves, but had hands and minds like people, would also be startled.

At least, that was the hope. Phase two didn't exactly depend on it, but the ability to startle these things was one of the less-documented subsets of phase two.

Not that phase two was complicated. In all honesty, calling it "phase two" was more a case of avoiding calling it "maybe this will actually work".

Happily...

...not happily. Nothing about this is happy...

...it worked.

They all jumped back in a wave, breaking the "creeping along" spell in the process.

Truth be told, Erin had startled herself at the scream. She had never tried to scream like that before, and it was a lot louder than she expected. A lot more effective.

She laughed.

She couldn't help it. It was the kind of laugh that bubbles up every time you suddenly realize something good. Whenever you solve a complicated problem, or pick a movie everybody likes. It was that kind of laugh. A type of disbelieving triumph.

Behind her, the door opened.

She jumped backward, keeping her eyes on the pack.

Hands and arms caught her, yanked her inside, and slammed the door.

Three seconds later, the first wolf hit the house.

When It's A Jar

It had been a good door. Solid oak, with more than a gallon of linseed oil rubbed into it over the past decade. It had been a loved door. A sturdy door. A luminous door.

Everything has its limits, though, and after a night of giant wolf things beating and chewing on it, the weak links were breaking down.

On the third impact, the door's top hinge sprang from the wall in a cloud of plaster dust. The next blow spun the door like a gyroscope, spiraling about the remaining hinge and the steel bolt.

Paws, then muzzles, then entire bodies pushed through. The pressure popped the last hinge apart with a metal ping, and the door collapsed to the floor.

At that exact moment, the window bars gave way to the pressure of bodies and tore from their wall mounts.

Howling gray death flooded into the cabin.

Pretty Dancing Lights

The room reeked of burning and gunfire and blood and meat. It filled their nostrils and swamped their brains with the urge to bite and claw and eat. It filled them with a frenzy.

The room was not as dark as the outside, so they could see that it was empty. A pile of furniture blocked a hallway, so several scrabbled at the pile to dislodge it.

The others filled the room.

A few investigated the tiny lights.

The tiny lights jumped and danced along the floor. The tiny lights skittered up the bookshelves, hopped along the kitchen countertops, and scurried across the walls.

Each tiny light hurried along toward its own pile of nearby taped-up sticks.

Thick red sticks that smelled wrong.

As the cabin flooded with wolves, the tiny dancing lights each finished their respective journeys.

For a fraction of a second, the room darkened.

Phase Three

Streak was glad to see the door come down and the bars in the windows collapse. The conflict between pack and blood hurt his head, and this would let them all move on to what they felt compelled to do.

The cabin lit up. Each window, bright as day. Perhaps brighter.

For an instant, Streak thought it was the blue lights again. There was almost a twinge of regret, because he thought for sure the blue light would be gone. Once things turned dim and stayed dim, the blue light stopped.

And then the cabin was gone. Not entirely gone, but replaced by a great shapeless boiling mass of white and orange and red.

Confusion flickered into the place where regret sat. There was something about this, something that alarmed Streak, something that triggered another memory.

A hot wind struck him and knocked him over, tumbling him up and down, tossed like a rat. He lost all orientation as he rolled, and his body felt hot and compressed and there was nothing to breathe but more hot.

A roar filled his ears until they rang, and then a hammer hit him and he heard nothing.

There was silence. Silence and pain.

Then came the darkness.

Packing Up

The howling. First thing he heard was the howling.

Streak snapped awake.

There was confusion, but it didn't last long.

The blood song came back, and with it came memories.

Understanding.

The cabin was nearly gone. Parts still stood, including a thick chunk in the middle, but the rest had vanished in the fireball.

Not vanished. Fragmented.

Streak walked into the wreckage. Body parts lay everywhere, some small, some large. Hair burnt off, sometimes skin, sometimes more.

There were confused howls, whines, snapping. There was pain.

This was not right, this was not going to work.

Streak moved from one to another, finding the lost, finding the hurt, and finding the confused. He let them know they weren't alone. He let them know there was still a pack and that they still belonged.

Creature by creature, the whining stopped. The whimpering stopped. The feeling of loss stopped.

They gathered in the clearing. They gathered and rejoined.

A Layered Approach

Streak circled the cabin.

Something else wasn't right. Something about this didn't make sense.

Three times he ran around, three times finding more wolves dazed and dizzy, eyes unfocused and confused, ears ringing from the explosion. He nosed them back to the pack and continued searching.

He found parts of wolves. He found wood. He found metal. But he didn't find what he was looking for.

He didn't find people.

Where were they?

On the fourth passage around, he stopped at the back door.

Miraculously, it still hung from a single hinge, even though most of its wall had collapsed.

Streak watched the door spin lazy on its remaining hinge.

He sat down.

Something was wrong.

He knew many had died in the explosion, but most remained. He heard their sounds on the other side of the wreckage. That sounded normal.

With a final creak, the door hinge gave way and fell to the still-warm dirt.

Streak looked at the door, at the dirt, at the paw prints in the dirt. Strange pawprints, with fingers digging in, and excellent sharp claws. Strange but effective. Streak knew they could do anything with paws like this. Anything they wanted—

What?

That flat spot.

That wasn't a pawprint. That was oval and flat.

It was a footprint. A shoeprint.

And it lay on top of the pawprints.

Pawprints first, footprints after.

Streak sprang up. Followed the footprint.

Another. And another.

Once he walked past the ring of pawprints, he saw more. Many more.

Streak looked from the ground, in the direction of the footprints.

That's when he saw the trail.

That's it!

He raised his head and howled. This wasn't a hurting howl or a succoring howl.

This was a hunting howl.

The pack answered. *His* pack answered.

Anger, pain, and confusion disappeared in the pulsing red howl of the hunt.

He led.

They followed.

Tranquility

The woods are a kind and gentle place where a person can find peace, seek their inner nature, and emerge renewed and ready to achieve great things after communing with a mystical earthy force.

Or, they are filled with hundreds of howling things that will tear your life to pieces, take over your living flesh, and transform you into one of their own, spreading and destroying all in your path.

On any given day, Carter might have figured option A was a safe bet. He had grown up in the hills above Los Angeles, so he had a lot of experience running around in the woods, following strange little game trails, and even spending long evenings under a blanket of unblinking beautiful stars. He had seen most every creature that wandered that mountainous area, including coyotes, wildcats, feral dogs, and even a few hermitty bums, and not under any circumstances had he ever felt in the slightest out of his depth as far as safety. Not once had he ever felt threatened, even when he saw the wildcat.

So, normally, option A.

But as they say, once someone becomes a man, they must put away childish things.

Apparently, none of those childish things should include the belief that random never-before-experienced creatures will appear and attack you. Option B becomes an *actual* option, instead of what we tell the younger siblings to keep them from following us out to our secret clubhouse we built from broken pallets.

The sky was turning pinkish-gray from the oncoming sun, but because most of the path was under a high and thick tree canopy, the party consisted of a line of flashlights bobbing along through the darkness.

In the lead, Carter stopped when he heard the howling. It wasn't the howling that had been happening after the cabin exploded. This sounded like the kind of howling they had heard earlier, when those things were following them.

Brass trundled by, even bulkier than normal in his dynamite vest.

"They're already following us," he said.

As Tom ran by, he asked "Why are you stopping?"

Jake, huffing, yanked on Carter's sleeve. "C'mon, keep running!" It seemed like a good idea, so Carter turned and followed.

Erin ran close behind.

Deadly Thread In A Dirty Needle

The trail was narrow. At most, two at a time could fit through it, so it took a while before they all made it through, but at least they all had the same purpose and the same direction again.

Hunting.

Focus On Low Impact

The boulders were as tall as she was, but at least the boulders on the path tended toward more reasonable step sizes.

Erin looked up.

About thirty feet up, Tom, Jake, and Carter were already topping the rock pile and starting in on the actual path that crisscrossed the mountainside. Brass was right behind them.

At least they weren't trying to climb this in the dark – the sky was still lightening in preparation for morning, but being out of the trees made it less dark.

"All clear?" she called out.

Jake looked down. "What are you doing down there?" he shouted. "You better haul ass – they're coming!"

Erin caught her breath and then heard the howling.

Time to be a scared little monkey, she thought. Instead of walking, or even running, she started jumping steps, including clambering up the higher blocks of rock on all fours. She had the advantage of everybody else at half the weight and half the age.

In a moment, she made the last jump and landed on the first ledge. Brass was there waiting for her, but the others had already started the climb. For a second, the weight of her pack threw her off and she windmilled her arms to regain balance, which would have worked except that something intercepted her arm and pulled her back upright.

It was Brass, who held her wrist.

"Be careful," he said.

"I had it," she protested.

"I'm sure you did," he said. "But I'm doing my best to keep you from banging dynamite against the rocks. I'm sure you understand."

Erin decided that in the future...

...assuming her future was longer than about half an hour...

...she would never chide anyone else who was trying to help. It made her sound like an asshole.

"What I meant to say was 'thanks'," she added, hoping it would be enough to cover her faux pas.

Brass grinned at her.

Recovery acceptable. Win!

They started running up the switchback trail.

Dimension Z

The bushes at the bottom of the boulders shook and half a dozen gray shapes ran out.

For a moment, they milled around the base of the rocks, unsure, and then one of them spotted the people climbing high above.

It bayed to the others and then the hunt was back on.

Uphill, Downhill, Bing-Bang-Boom

Still trailing, Erin heard the wolves hit the open area. In the lightening sky, she saw the shapes at the bottom of the hill swirl around the rocks, and then file up the narrow trail.

"Time for a test!" she called out.

The others turned to look.

She gripped one of her dynamite sticks.

Please don't blow me up, she thought. *Please do what you're supposed to be doing and light nicely, so that I can throw you away and hear you go boom.*

She pulled.

With a hiss, the stick came loose from the bundle. The fuse, eight inches long, burned quickly along the length.

I am throwing lit sticks of dynamite. I am doing something that I never thought I would do. This is like a video game. It's the most surreal thing ever. I guess I'm ready to learn how to fish now.

"Fire in the hole!" she shouted, and threw the dynamite.

It spun in the air on its way down, the smoke from the fuse forming a wavy arc.

It wedged itself right on the path, three feet in front of a running wolf.

She watched the thing take a leap over the stick. As its body obscured the fuse, everything exploded.

She turned away from looking, but her last impression was of a wolf-shaped expanding shadow above an orange ball of fire.

If I think too hard about what I'm wearing, I will one hundred percent lose my shit.

She tried to not think about it, and kept running.

Test successful.

Taking A Breather

Erin rounded a corner and Jake was there, leaning over, hands on his knees, panting.

"You go on ahead," he said. "I need a breather. I'm not used to running anywhere, much less uphill, much less wearing a parka of doom."

She stopped.

Looked down the path.

"Here," she said. "Let's give you more of a breather than that."

She pulled another stick of dynamite. Smoke danced from the tip of the fuse.

She flung it out and it dropped past their line of sight.

A dull whomping sound signaled the detonation. A chorus of yelps followed.

"Now *that's* a breather," she said.

He raised an eyebrow.

"Maybe it wasn't such a good idea introducing you to explosives," he said.

"Pandora couldn't close her box, either," she replied with a shrug. "Besides, I'm small and weak, so I can't throw rocks. Dynamite is better."

He grinned. "Yeah, I suppose it is. It's a lot of rock-bang, all crammed into an easy-throw stick."

"You know it."

The howling started again.

"You ready, sir?"

He nodded and they continued up.

The Coefficient of Static Friction

Above them stretched a thin path, switchbacking against the wall of a long flat sloping rock.

About halfway up, Erin turned. Jake was still out of breath, but keeping time.

"This is a good position," she said. "We can keep tossing dynamite on them forever from here. You would have time for a breather and a nice hot cup of tea. Maybe even catch a movie before we ran out of boom."

"Yeah, that would be nice, but I think we better settle their hash before we start celebrating."

"I guess you have a point. Still, it's an appealing idea, throwing dynamite at werewolves."

"It surely is," said Jake.

He caught up with her and stretched his back.

"How high does this go?" she asked. "I see one path. Does it turn back?" He looked wrung out. She turned to look upward. She couldn't see the others due to a bend in the rocks.

"This is the last section of the trail. The mine's right around the – *shit!*"

All Erin heard was a scraping of rock.

Just as she turned, she saw Jake, his arms whirling, fall backwards off the edge of the cliff.

"*JAKE!*"

He was gone.

Only Solutions

Allegedly, when you fall, time slows down.

Maybe that's when you're young, though.

Jake realized he had slipped from the path when the rocky ground smashed into him. There was a loud crack from inside his hip.

Then he was in the air again, freefalling.

Goddammit, I bounced, he thought. *I didn't know I could bounce.*

Ten feet further down, he landed on his feet. His legs refused to work, however, and he collapsed and rolled another five feet further down the trail.

Almost as if he planned it, he landed on his ass right smack in the middle of the trail. Upright. Conscious.

Pain blasted through him – his head and his shoulders and his arms. Not his legs, though. He felt nothing from his legs. He looked down at them, but they were folded and twisted under him.

Sticks and stones did break my bones, he thought. Then he realized that the two sticks he saw *were* bones. *Not good. Not good at all.*

He heard the growling.

Looked to the left – downhill. The act of turning his head made a hundred little lights go off in his vision, and made his neck feel like someone was trying to tear it off with a chain.

Also, probably not good.

"Damn," he managed to croak.

He had landed ahead of most of the pack. Not far ahead, though. Maybe fifteen feet.

He had startled them enough that they had stopped their running.

Well, he thought, *no better time than the present.*

He reached for a stick of dynamite.

The fingers of his left hand were bent backwards. The last two fingers hung from a thick thread.

He closed his eyes a moment and let the nausea pass.

He tried to bring his right hand up, but it refused to move. *Okay, left it is, then,* he thought.

He bit his lip and looked closer.

He could move his thumb. He could move his thumb enough to make a pincher against the meat of what was left of his hand.

That's how we solve problems, he thought. *Good ol' American know-how, and opposable thumbs.*

His hand shivered, but he was able to pinch it around a stick of dynamite.

Blood made the stick slippery. He pinched hard with his thumb, and that pressed against the half of his hand that was no longer a functional hand anymore, but felt more like about a pound of angry nerves.

That's the pain I was expecting, he thought, once the flash of agony died down enough for a coherent thought.

"Jake!"

He heard her voice, way, way far away.

Oh, don't you even think of coming down here after me, he thought. *I'm about as broken as a man can get without actually checking out.*

Somehow, that thought brought him comfort. He realized at that moment that he wasn't trying to survive or to get away – there was no hope of that.

The wolves were closer. He could see their teeth and hear their growls.

You guys get to me, and sure, I'll get better, and I'll be able to move around again, but then I won't be me anymore. I'll be one of you. And, no offense, but as they say in the movies, fuck that noise.

Despite the pain, he managed to yank a stick of dynamite out of his pack.

Doggie wanna stick? Wanna play fetch? Wanna—

He stared at his hand, confused. There was no stick of dynamite clenched in his battered mitt. His bloody thumb held nothing ready to throw.

But he could hear the fuse.

He looked down into his lap.

Oh, he thought.

There you are.

And then he realized what he had been trying to do.

His world went hot and white and then black and forever.

The Diamond

She saw it all.

She saw him fall, she saw him bounce and spin.

She saw his legs flop as he rolled, and she saw him come to a stop, dirt- and blood-streaked.

She saw the wolves come closer.

She called his name – impulsively – and she saw him try to look up.

She saw him try to pull the dynamite from his vest and she saw – before he did – what happened.

She saw the first flash and ducked back. She closed her eyes, thinking that this would keep her from seeing more.

When the rest of his backpack went off, she felt the tremor under feet, and she felt airborne things striking her.

Even with her eyes closed, she saw what happened.

When it was done and there was silence, she still wouldn't look down, but she saw anyway.

What she saw changed her forever.

After the whining and whimpering from below stopped and the howling started again, she opened her eyes, but she was not the same person who closed them.

She ran.

Studying For The Finals

"Seriously, duct tape?" Carter watched Tom crisscross another yard of silver tape to the pile of dynamite sticks.

"We're in a hurry, and it sticks to anything," said Tom. "What more do you want?"

Three dynamite backpacks duct-taped to support beams now decorated the inside of the mineshaft. More sticks were taped to the low ceiling. Sticks were, in fact, jammed into every nook and crack within five feet of the entrance.

Wire detonators connected everything to a single box just inside the doorway.

Brass ran up, a length of wire in his hands. "It's all set up behind that big boulder there," he said. "Should protect us, but that means we've got to make sure everything's arranged perfectly when we set it off."

"What do you mean perfectly?" asked Carter.

Brass looked at him. "The wolves need to be inside the mine, we need to be outside of the mine, and the boulder has to be between us and anything that's going to go boom."

Carter shook his head. "That's not what I – oh, nevermind."

Then they heard it.

They had been hearing the occasional *foom* of the stray stick of dynamite, but this was different. This was deeper and throatier. This shook the ground and made the birds fly from the trees below, complaining in their shrill voices about the early morning.

All three looked back in the direction they came.

The pink dawn sky illuminated the plain at the top of the mine entrance. It was a flat space the size of a small house, strewn with boulders and rocks, some large as a car.

Twenty yards away, next to that biggest boulder, the path that brought them here spiraled down the mountainside.

"That was more than a stick," said Tom.

"Oh god," said Carter.

There was silence for a few seconds – nothing but the dim echoes of the detonation returning from the opposite wall of the valley.

And then the howls returned.

Each man looked at one another.

Carter shook his head. "I don't know, I don't know," he said. "What the fuck. Why are we even bothering? I mean, c'mon, do we really think we can—"

"Hey!"

Erin ran into view from behind the ridge. The instant she saw them, she ran over.

Out of breath, she staggered. Brass caught her.

"We lost him," she said. "We lost Jake."

"Shit," said Carter.

"I presume they're still following you?" asked Tom.

She nodded.

"Okay then, we better get you out of that pack and get it wired in with the rest," he said.

A howl broke the morning air.

She shrugged off the backpack, but walked past Tom. She wedged it against the floor, next to a few other sticks. "I don't think it needs to be wired into anything," she said. "Peer pressure ought to do the trick."

Another howl, and now they could hear the claws against gravel and the growling.

"Should we hide?" asked Carter.

"No," said Erin. "They'll find us if we hide. They'll spread out and look for us. We want them all inside, and that means they have to see us go in."

"Are you sure?" asked Carter. "Because we don't know what's really in there. I mean, what if it doesn't loop, what if it's a dead end after all? What if we go in and it's fifty feet long, and collapsed already?"

243

Erin straightened up. She exchanged a silent glance with Brass.

She turned to Tom. "You have a lighter?" she asked.

He fished around in his pocket, then produced one. Handed it to her.

She stepped to her backpack, and extracted a single stick of dynamite.

She looked at the other three.

"We are all going into that mine," she said. "And they are all going to follow us in. If the mine loops, then we try to trick them into going the wrong way and we escape and blow the shit out of the mine. If the mine doesn't split, then we wait until they are all inside and we blow the shit out of the mine anyway. This is the plan. Right now."

She jammed the stick of dynamite into one pocket and the lighter into another.

Tom shrugged. "Sounds like crap, but I can't do any better."

No one else spoke.

The first wolf cleared the lip of the ridge.

In The Moist Dark Places
Filled With Things That Creepeth

One flashlight.

All they had was one flashlight.

Carter led the way. Behind him Tom, then Erin, then Brass.

In the movies, the inside of a mine is dry, sometimes dusty. Maybe there are rail tracks, perhaps a friendly well-oiled cart that the heroes can climb into and ride.

Hatchet Mine was not a movie type of mine. Hatchet Mine was a dank and nasty place. Most of the floor was covered in slimy water. The water gave the illusion of a level floor, but the floor was anything but. Rocks and pits and chunks of not-fully-rotten wooden ties tripped them at every step.

The walls of the mine were jagged hooks of rock that shimmered and danced in the flashlight's combination of weak illumination and stark crazy shadows.

At one point, Erin stumbled over a rock and threw her hand against a wall to catch herself. She caught herself, but when her hand hit the wall, it didn't feel like rock.

It crunched and rippled.

Without thinking, she jumped back and an involuntary cry popped out.

Carter turned the flashlight back at her.

"What the fuck's on the wall?"

"Oh," said Carter. "Some kind of cricket. Sorry I didn't say anything earlier. Don't touch the wall. I don't think they're poisonous or anything."

She shuddered. "Crickets?! But they're huge!"

"Yeah. Kinda gross."

She had a thought pass through her mind that as they went deeper into this mine, the crickets would get larger and then eventually, the mine would open up and they would be in a subterranean world filled with dinosaurs. Or giant crickets. One or the other.

245

Then Tom yanked on her shirt. "C'mon, quit dozing," he said, and they continued running through the water.

No dinosaurs today.

"How far in is the fork?" she asked. "Hey Carter, you see anything yet?"

"Nope," came the reply. "Just walls on the left and walls on the right and a big-ass hole straight down the middle."

"Keep looking," said Tom. "Didn't he say it was a hundred yards in or so?"

"Yeah, but that was crazy-mountain-man yards, which for all I know is eight miles," said Carter. "No offense, but if you think we can go any faster without breaking our necks, you are welcome to take point."

"Just keep going," said Erin. "Maybe it gets easier the further in we go."

"You keep telling yourself that," laughed Carter.

Light Gambling

They gathered at the mouth of the mine, swirling up from the trail, but refusing to go in.

They knew the people had all gone in, but it was dark. Darker than the night. Darker than anything they had seen. And they didn't have the keen eyes they had expected to. Not even ordinary wolves could see in that dark.

So they piled up at the entrance.

Finally, Streak arrived.

He saw the flat plateau.

He ran its half-circumference, and was sure that no one hid anywhere. He was sure they had all gone into the mine, into the hole in the ground.

It was dark, true. Very dark.

But he knew they were in there. He saw the footprints in the mud near the first puddle. He saw all the things they left behind. He could even hear them.

He growled at the others, nipped at the nearest one, and then ran inside. The only thing they could do was try to be careful. If the people had lights, then it was important to catch up to them as soon as possible. If the people didn't have lights, then they were also going slow.

So, going fast was the solution.

When Streak ran, the others followed.

Within ninety seconds, every remaining wolf was threading deep into the heart of Hatchet Mine.

A Definite Sense Of Unexpected Intimacy

The first howl shocked them all into stillness. Unlike the other howls, it wasn't a distinct sound. It was a rumbling overlapping call that echoed up and back. It sounded like eight million wolves ten feet behind.

"Holy shit," said Carter. "How close are they?"

"I assume they just came in," said Erin. "Sound carries in here, and once they're inside the walls, there's nowhere for it to go but forward. So they're not that close."

"Not that we have time for a picnic," said Tom. "Maybe the water will slow them down a little."

"Right," said Carter. "Water may be their natural enemy." He pressed on.

Re-Org

Streak was unsure.

To be clear, Streak was sure of some things and not sure of other things.

Streak was sure the people lay in this direction. Absolutely sure. He could hear them.

What he wasn't sure about was everything else. He wasn't sure about what this all meant, why they were hiding in a hole. He wasn't sure why they left all their things back at the mouth of the mine.

Streak's brain tried to work the puzzle out, but it was a tiny bit too complicated for him.

That didn't mean he didn't know that something wasn't right. So far, every time something hadn't felt right, there had been bad things following. This felt no different except that in this case, there was nowhere else to go, no other decision that could be made.

Streak slowed down. Not much, but enough to let the wolf immediately behind him pass. Then he let another pass. Then another and another.

It wasn't long before he was at the back of the pack.

This felt safer, somehow. This felt better.

Everything still felt terribly, terribly wrong, but at least now, Streak could see options.

One Man's Trash

"Check it out!" crowed Carter.

"You find the fork yet?"

"No, just some stuff."

The tunnel had been widened here. A kind of kiosk had been cut into the side of the wall, and some random bits of wood and metal scrap had been left behind.

"I guess that's the closest thing to treasure we were going to find," muttered Tom. "Some shitty tools and shitty wood and shitty puddles of water."

"Don't forget shitty crickets," added Erin.

"Hey," said Brass. "They're catching up fast."

Tom raised his head and listened to the rumbled baying of the wolves behind them. "He's right. I don't know where the fork is, but we aren't going to make it. We're too damn slow. Maybe we better get ready?"

Carter looked around. "No, no," he said. "I think it loops soon. It can't be far."

His brain churned and then his eyes lit up.

"Okay, I have an idea. Quick, go there. Look in that hole. Is there anything big, like a pallet or sheet or plywood or anything?" he shined the light over Tom's shoulder.

Tom looked through the scraps. "Mostly rotten shit. Some cable, and a couple of – oh, here you go!" He pulled out a piece of plywood.

Black mold mottled it and it was already starting to rot itself apart, but it could be held up.

"Perfect! Okay, this is what I think you guys should do. Get into that little hole and pull the plywood in front of you."

"We won't all fit," said Brass.

"You don't have to all fit, you just have to set it so that they run past you." He held the plywood at an angle, hinging it in the direction of the mouth of the mine, but open in the direction they were running. "As long as you don't move, they'll probably not even notice you."

He turned to Erin. "Are you *sure* they can't smell?"

"I'm here, aren't I?" she asked.

Carter shrugged. "Okay, fine. Then stay low. Here, let me help get that set up." He adjusted the plywood. "You guys stay here until they all pass, then run back to the entrance. Get ready to blow this shit up. I'll run and lose them in the loop, and meet you at the surface."

"You think they're going to follow you?" asked Tom.

"Oh, they *will* be following me for a little while, but then they won't be because then they'll be following what they *think* is me," said Carter. He fished into his pocket and pulled out a chemical light. Cracked it and shook it. A green light filled the room. "What they're *really* going to follow is the light."

He hurled the light further down the tunnel. "By the time they reach this spot, they're gonna be starved for light, so they'll head right to it. Away from you. Toward the loop. Trust me – I worked this all out in the last ninety seconds, so it's foolproof."

"You had that all the time and you made us use only one light?" asked Erin.

Carter shrugged. "I didn't know how deep the mine was," he said. "And I didn't want all our lights to go out at once. Besides," he nodded at Tom. "He has a lighter. You'll be fine. Now get down!"

He pushed them low, arranged the plywood, and ran down the tunnel.

The Skipper

The floor of the mine was dry enough here to not have puddles, although Carter still danced around to avoid tripping over rocks or clocking his skull against protrusions.

The flashlight helped a little, but also made things more challenging. Long, sharp shadows jerked around with each running step he took.

C'mon, fork in the road! C'mon, c'mon, c'mon!

A Dark Silence In The Dark Noise

The howling grew louder.

Be still. Be quiet. Be nothing.

Erin knew this was what worked in the woods, so it should work here, too.

Then again, maybe not.

Maybe they had crappy eyesight and crappy hearing and a crappy sense of smell, but all of that happened in the big open tree- and scent-filled woods, with a single terrified person trying to hide.

Here, there were three sweaty terrified people, crammed into a much smaller space, all inside a narrow tunnel.

So, maybe all bets were off.

Only thing she *could* control was making herself small and invisible. Erin closed her eyes.

Be nothing.

The howling came closer.

In the confines of the rock walls, the echoes doubled and redoubled on themselves so much that there was no distinct howling anymore, only a wall of sound.

And they're not even here yet, she thought.

There was a brief temptation to put her fingers in her ears, knowing it was going to get louder and louder, but that would have meant moving. Right now, moving was out of the question.

Invisible people didn't move.

Crossroad Sweetening

The fork!

Carter skidded to a stop.

Which way to go, which way to go?

One of the forks looked smoother and easier for running, but it wasn't quite as straight-up from the main shaft. The fork that was more a continuation of the shaft looked rougher.

He needed to make sure that they ran down only one of the forks – not both.

He took a few steps down one side, and then a few steps down another.

The howling grew louder. The howling shifted in pitch and some other quality he couldn't quite put his finger on, but he knew what it meant.

They had found the first chemical light.

He decided.

Carter stepped into the straighter tunnel, dancing over the rocks on the floor. At about fifteen feet in, he stopped.

Reached into his pocket, and pulled out another chemical light.

Cracked it and shook it.

Green light filled the tunnel. If he had a minute, he would have marveled at the surreal appearance.

He set the light on a flat rock. Enough to fill the cavern and lead the poor doggies astray. Enough to distract them from the darker side tunnel.

He skipped back over the rocks to the beginning of the fork, and crept about six feet down inside the other branch. As the tunnel cricked left, he crouched down.

He could still see into the area where the tunnel forked, as the chemical light lit that whole branch.

Please fall for this trick again, you dumb-ass dogs, he thought.

Crashing Waves

They had arrived.

The chemical light Carter had first thrown down the shaft served its purpose beautifully.

As soon as the wolves saw the distant green, they were encouraged and doubled their speed toward it.

In doing so, they completely ignored the bulging section of wall in the form of a piece of plywood. Ignoring that, they never saw the three people crouched behind it.

Although the green light was dim and distant, it was bright enough to light most of the tunnel.

Even behind the plywood, there was enough wan green light leaking into the darkness for Erin to make out the shapes of the faces of her companions and their eyes reflecting in the dark.

She shuddered a little, even though she knew these were friends. Those green points of reflection on dark faces was pegging the scale of her weird-o-meter, and this was even after a night of fighting off bloodthirsty werewolves.

Behind the points of light, she knew those eyes held the same thing her eyes held.

Raw wild terror.

There were no real sensations anymore.

At first, the howling of the beasts as they passed was so loud it rang in their ears, but now, after a few minutes, it was a buzzing, wavering semi-deafness experienced by everyone.

The occasional passing body bumping sideways into the plywood was a moment of adrenalin-flooded panic, but after a few minutes, the rhythms of the impacts felt more like a strange rolling ocean, raised vertically instead of lying flat on the ground like a proper ocean.

The constant sensory flood overwhelmed their senses, and they crouched behind the plywood as wave after wave of monster passed by, hoping that none of the passing creatures saw or heard or smelled anything.

It was hard to hold out hope in the middle of this thunderous storm, but somehow, they managed.

Special Deliverance

Finally, the wave slowed.

Finally, they were able to make out individuals.

Finally, the sounds faded into the distance.

It wasn't silent, but there was no sound from nearby.

Erin counted to ten in her head, barely breathing.

Still no sound.

She turned her head toward Brass. In the dim light, her eyes adjusted enough to see him better. Shapes and contours.

She could tell he was watching her and listening to the animal sounds at the same time.

She raised an eyebrow.

He shook his head the tiniest amount.

Like the gentlest spider ever created, his fingertips followed her pant leg down to her ankle. Reached under. Withdrew her "letter opener."

Through all of this, he never made a sound she could hear.

She felt him tense.

She also tensed up, but compared to him, she was thin and hardly a wisp. When Brass tensed, he was made out of rock in a human skin.

He stepped out from behind the plywood.

From her vantage point, Erin heard the tiniest clatter of claws on rock, but she saw Brass swing a fist and she heard it connect with something that cracked and yowled.

She stood up to see better. *Probably not the smartest thing I ever did,* she thought as she did it, but it was too late now to stop.

There was one wolf and it was still crumpled across the other end of the tunnel, recovering from Brass's punch.

It found its feet and scrabbled upright.

At first, it looked at Brass, murder in its eyes, and then it saw her.

You!

It was the one. The leader. The wolf with the streak across its face.

Its eyes glowed in hot fury and it leaped – not at Brass, but at Erin.

In the dim green light, Brass swung his fist down in a blur. It connected with the wolf's head.

The power of it drove the thing right to the floor, chin-first.

Where it stayed.

The hilt of Erin's knife protruded from its skull.

Together, they watched as the last seconds of its life twitched away.

Brass reached down and pulled the knife out of its shattered skull.

Wiped it clean on the neck fur, and then his own pants leg.

Handed it hilt-first back to her.

"No time to ask politely. Sorry, boss." he said.

She grinned, took the knife, and slipped it back into the hilt. "No problem."

Tom stood up. "Okay, we have to run. You remember that, right?"

They ran.

Reunion

The wolves flowed like an ocean.

From within a shadow, in the dark corner of the fork the beasts ignored, Carter watched the ocean of snarling gray follow his lure and then follow each other.

Eventually, the last straggler passed by.

Carter grinned in the dark.

"I did good, baby," he whispered.

He stood up.

His shadow wavered in front of him.

Shadow?

He turned.

Behind him, the tunnel was filled with monsters, each gray face hungry and each pair of eyes cold in the reflection from the chemical light one held in its teeth.

It dropped the light at his feet, but its mouth remained open.

"I really did."

They fell upon him.

He didn't scream once.

Short Circuited

Streaks of sunlight crept through the trees of the distant eastern mountain range. It wasn't quite full daylight, but full daylight was about to make an appearance any minute.

Erin, Brass, and Tom stumbled out of the mine, shading their eyes against the brilliant sunlight that wasn't there yet.

Tom drew his gun first and spun, hoping he wouldn't have to use it against any stray wolves, on account of the fact that he was having a lot of trouble adjusting to the glare of daylight.

Brass ran to the biggest boulder.

Erin blinked away the sparkling in her eyes and the threatening headache.

"Is it okay?" she asked.

Brass nodded. "Ready when you are, boss."

She and Tom ran over.

"We're waiting for Carter," she said.

"Of course we're waiting for Carter," repeated Tom.

"You hear him?"

He closed his eyes and concentrated. "I don't. But that doesn't mean he's not coming. Do you hear him?"

She listened. "No."

Brass wired the detonator. Calling it a detonator was a bit of an exaggeration. It was a skeletal wall light switch in a plastic box.

"Any time," he said.

Tom watched the mine entrance. "I don't see him yet."

They crouched behind the rock, watching.

"I hear something," Brass whispered.

Then the others heard it too.

Howling.

260

Zero Contact

Erin stood up. "*Carter!*" she yelled.

The howling intensified.

"Shit, he's gone," said Tom. He turned to Brass. "Blow it."

Brass looked at Erin and she nodded.

He flipped the switch.

Nothing happened.

He flipped the switch back and forth a couple of times.

Not one stick of dynamite exploded in response.

Tom squinted at the mouth of the mine.

The howling was getting louder.

"What happened?" asked Erin.

"Shit, it pulled loose. I can see it from here," said Tom.

He turned to Brass. "Turn that off." Turned to Erin. "I'm only doing this once."

He ran to the mouth of the mine.

The leads lay on the ground, about a foot away from where they pulled free of the connector.

Closure

Tom slid to his knees and pulled the wires back toward the connector.

They came up short.

He could hear the wolves in the dark, the howling, the hunger, and the splashing of their feet as they raced toward the circle of white sunlight.

"Give me a foot!" he called out.

It wasn't going to work. He wasn't going to be able to do it.

He held the wires ready. One had been connected already.

He closed his eyes.

His heart beat.

If he ran now, sideways from the mouth of the mine, he might make it. He might manage to escape from the things in the mine if none of them saw him run.

But they would still be free, and they would still spread.

He knew this.

He also knew if he made the connection, he would not make it clear of the blast. There was enough dynamite there to blast him to pieces if he weren't hidden behind a boulder. Like the others were.

Those are some shit-ass choices, he thought. *But really, had there ever been a choice?*

"Fuck," he muttered.

"*Do it!*" he screamed. "*Switch it on! NOW!*"

He could almost see them in the depths of the mine. Almost see eyes bouncing.

"Nothing's happening!" shouted Erin back.

"Just making sure," he muttered.

He shoved the second wire into the connector. There was a tiny electrical snap.

And then there was a flash of light.

In the flash of light, he saw the things not ten feet from the mine's mouth. The front one was in mid-leap, mouth open, tongue hanging out.

Then the light was gone, replaced by heat, and some kind of roaring and darkness.

Tongue of Flame

They weren't ready. They wanted to be ready, but they had been standing when Tom called out and there was no time to collapse.

The shock wave blew them down.

The tongue of flame and heat and debris from the mouth of the mine passed across the top of the boulder, transforming the pink morning sky into a hellish wave of flaming plasma.

And then it was gone. It was all gone.

Benediction

The morning sun continued rising.

Having cleared the eastern range, its warm rays fell upon the plateau that used to be the mouth of Hatchet Mine. The mine was gone, however. The mouth collapsed and a broad section of the mountain above had slipped loose and fallen down, further covering the entrance.

There was no more Hatchet Mine.

There was a slab of broken rock over a pile of small boulders.

If there was anything else, it was gone forever from the world.

Walkers

The woods were quiet.

She stepped out from between the trees. Soot and sweat streaked her face and her hair stood up in the air, singed in places.

Two bandoliers crossed her shoulders, heavy with ammunition as the shoulder pack she wore.

The bushes rustled and he stepped out next to her. His compact frame wore even more supplies.

The bolt hole had been the most secure room in the cabin. Perfect for storing weapons. For whoever came back.

Together, they looked at the top of the mountain. Smoke spiraled above it in the still morning air.

"I suppose," said Erin. "That we ought to follow the road back."

"Like the man said, only way out," said Brass.

They started walking.

"I hate the outdoors," muttered Erin.

"Right there with you, boss."

Just then, in the distance, a rolling boom cracked though the air.

They stopped.

Looked at each other.

"Other end of the valley," said Brass. "Not us."

Erin nodded. "Yeah, you're right," she said. "But I have a feeling it might not hurt to check it out."

"I have a feeling you're right."

They cinched their packs and kept walking.

the end

The Publisher

Hellbender Media (HellbenderMedia.com) offers rare and voracious entertainment for the reader who prefers the Unusual, including books, movies, games, and other fun things, as well as offering workshops, tutorials, and lots of interactivity with their fans.

Hellbender Media includes these and other strange products:

The DVD adaptation of one of the most amazing fantasy novels ever written.

A collection of bizarre short movies, composed entirely of 100% fun.

A 10-minute parody of the entire trilogy, hilariously told with... er, "puppets."

A short adaptation of one of Lovecraft's most intriguing tales.

The Author

Edward Martin III is a writer, an essayist, and an award-winning filmmaker from Portland, OR. He adapted and directed an animated adaptation of H. P. Lovecraft's *The Dream-Quest of Unknown Kadath*, produced *The Cosmic Horror Fun-Pak*, wrote and directed a 10-minute comprehensive period adaptation of *Lord of the Rings*, and is in deep post-production of *Flesh of my Flesh*, a ground-breaking independent zombie action movie. He's also in development or preproduction for several other feature films, and a handful of shorts.

Edward's first book *Close Your Eyes: tales from the Blinkspace* sold nearly four or five copies before Good Taste set in, but if this book left you wondering how a good man can be led astray by a wily typewriter, then please, by all means, check out *Close Your Eyes: tales from the Blinkspace*, at the nearest disreputable bookstore to you. He is seeking help, rest assured.

Visit **HellbenderMedia.com** for more information.

The Last Word

I never expected to write *Through the Night*. Right up until the first day I started writing it, if you had asked me if I was going to write this novel, I would have said "Nope – no need to. There's a movie coming out."

But I realized three important things. In least order of significance:

First, the movie might not come out. It's true, as much as people out there think Hollywood has movies flying out like some kind of infernal spray, the harsh fact is that there are thousands of scripts and hundreds of movies that will never ever be finished or come out if they are. No one knows how this labyrinthine charnel house works. Magic or something.

Second, the movie might not come out, but would be different. This is so common, it's a running joke. I've even made a short movie that makes fun of this exact process: *ManSlugs! the making of 'a Sci-Fi Original'*. In that movie, the hapless writer watches in horror as her wonderful script is slowly whittled and compromised down until there is only the vaguest shell remaining. Will that happen to *Through the Night*? I don't know. Probably. I mean, I'm not independently wealthy, so that means I depend on those who are, and they have demands and such.

Finally, the movie wasn't the whole story. Probably the bottom line in this is that there are a lot of things going on that never could make it in the script, that never could work in the movie. There are thoughts and feelings and fears and worries that we will never see. But they are there, and I can bring them out where you can see them. Here in this book, you can understand more about those moments where Jake's exterior reveals a crack, or why Deedee acts the way she does, and how terrified she (and all of us) are when the tools that we have always used stop working. There was more. Much more.

So, all of a sudden, I'm writing this book.

In a very Dread Pirate Roberts way, I kept looking at the manuscript every night and saying "I'll probably blow you off tomorrow. Too busy to write."

That, of course, was just dumb. I'm *never* too busy to write. I was lyin' like a rug to myself.

I hope you enjoyed *Through the Night*. If you do, please let me know. Writing is a crazy passionate disturbing process, but no matter how intense writers get, a fan letter makes them dance around like that imaginary baby on Ally McBeal. If *that* cultural reference doesn't terrify you, I can see I have my work cut out for me.

And yes, I have something else planned. Something very exciting.

www.ingramcontent.com/pod-product-compliance
Lightning Source LLC
Chambersburg PA
CBHW070659280626
47159CB00022B/1004